Julia Gillian

(and the Quest for Joy)

by Alison McGhee

with pictures by Drazen Kozjan

SCHOLASTIC INC.

New York   Toronto   London   Auckland
Sydney   Mexico City   New Delhi   Hong Kong

No part of this publication may be reproduced, stored in a retrieval system, or transmitted in any form or by any means, electronic, mechanical, photocopying, recording, or otherwise, without written permission of the publisher. For information regarding permission, write to Scholastic Inc., Attention: Permissions Department, 557 Broadway, New York, NY 10012.

This book was originally published in hardcover by Scholastic Press in 2009.

ISBN 978-0-545-03352-7

Text copyright © 2009 by Alison McGhee.
Illustrations copyright © 2009 by Drazen Kozjan.
All rights reserved. Published by Scholastic Inc.
SCHOLASTIC, APPLE, APPLE SERIES, and associated logos
are trademarks and/or registered trademarks of Scholastic Inc.

12 11 10 9 8 7 6 5 4   11 12 13 14 15/0

Printed in the U.S.A.   40
First Scholastic paperback printing, July 2010

TO DEVON O'BRIEN

—A.M.

FOR LYDIA AND SABRINE

—D.K.

ACKNOWLEDGMENTS

My huge thanks to Kara LaReau, editor, whose keen and loving eye guided this book every step of the way. Thanks also to Abby Ranger, whose insider scoop on the art of trumpeting was invaluable, and to Marijka Kostiw, whose eye for book design is astonishing. Thanks and love to Brad Zellar, for his help on this and other books, and to Min O'Brien, first reader, whose smirks and chuckles made me smile.

CHAPTER ONE

How Now Brown Cows?

It was the end of September, and Julia Gillian, along with the other Lake Harriet Elementary School students, had been in school for nearly a month. At lunchtime, Julia Gillian headed straight for the table where she and her best friend, Bonwit Keller, usually sat. Bonwit was already there, along with Cerise Cronin and Lathrop Fallon, the two other friends who sat at their lunch table.

"How now brown cows?" said Julia Gillian.

How now brown cow was one of Julia Gillian's favorite phrases, and even though it didn't sound quite the same when pluralized, she still liked the way it rolled off her tongue.

"This brown cow is happy that it's finally lunchtime," said Cerise grimly.

Cerise, who was not a fan of school, had long proclaimed that her favorite subjects were lunch and recess.

"Well, this brown cow thought the morning went by fast," said Bonwit. "It's hard to believe that it's lunchtime already."

"You *would* think the morning went by fast," said Cerise.

Bonwit had always liked school, and so — with the exception of Reading — did Julia Gillian. Much as it pained her schoolteacher parents, who believed that a love of books was the cornerstone to a good education, Julia Gillian did not enjoy reading. There was much to be happy about anyway at Lake Harriet Elementary. Bonwit and Julia Gillian were both in Ms. Schultz's fifth-grade class, which meant that they spent the entire day together.

Mrs. K, who had been their lunch lady for many years, came down the aisle between the tables. Mrs. K was beloved among the Lake Harriet students. She was a dog lover, which was reason enough to like her, and she walked about the lunchroom with the help of a cane topped with a carved wooden dog's head.

"Hello, Mrs. K," said Julia Gillian. "I like your dog-head cane."

She said this to Mrs. K every day. It was their routine.

"Hello, Julia Gillian," said Mrs. K. "You're a true dog person, aren't you?"

It was a known fact that Julia Gillian was indeed a true dog person. She and her St. Bernard, Bigfoot, were almost exactly the same age. Julia Gillian could barely remember a day in her life without Bigfoot, who was her constant companion. He slept in her room on a long magenta pillow with his stuffed bat under his chin, and every day they went for a walk through the streets of their south Minneapolis neighborhood.

"Indeed I am, Mrs. K," said Julia Gillian.

Mrs. K winked at Julia Gillian, and Julia Gillian winked back. She was not very good at winking, but practice made perfect, and every day she practiced winking with the help of Mrs. K. She hoped to be able to add "Skilled at the Art of Winking" soon to the ongoing list of accomplishments that she kept in a notebook under her mattress.

There were many good things about being a Lake Harriet student, including Mrs. K. An especially good thing was that today was the first day of music lessons. Julia Gillian and Bonwit had been looking forward to studying the trumpet since they were kindergartners, and finally their day had arrived. The music teacher, Mr. Mixler, was one of the most popular teachers at Lake Harriet. Julia Gillian was already looking forward to adding "Skilled at the Art of the Trumpet" to her list of accomplishments. Her parents, who were fans of jazz music, had also been looking forward to her trumpet lessons.

"What's it like there in Bonwit World, where school always goes by fast?" said Cerise.

She tapped her forehead and squinted in a quizzical manner, imitating Bonwit.

"I don't know, exactly," said Bonwit, who treated all questions with his usual seriousness. "I mean, I've been living in Bonwit World all my life."

Cerise rolled her eyes. All the fifth-graders had been together since the first day of kindergarten, and they knew each other well, so Bonwit was not hurt by Cerise's eye-rolling. For a moment, Julia Gillian considered Cerise's question. What, in fact, would it be like to be Bonwit? He was serious, Cerise was sarcastic, Lathrop was always a bit behind everyone else, and Julia Gillian was . . . well, she was Julia Gillian. While most of the time Julia Gillian enjoyed being herself, there were times when it was a bit boring, being the same person day in and day out. It might be fun to be someone else, if only for a short time.

Julia Gillian and Bonwit walked down the hall to Mr. Mixler's room for their first trumpet lesson. It was exciting to think that by next month at this time, they might actually be playing the trumpet. Mr. Mixler would soon be teaching them "Let's Go, Band!" or "Song of My Soul," which were two of the first songs studied by Lake Harriet Elementary musicians.

"Which do you like better, marches or jazz?" said Bonwit.

"Jazz."

"Me too."

"Maybe, if we get good enough, we can be famous jazz trumpeters," said Julia Gillian.

"And tour the world together," said Bonwit.

"Maybe we'll get standing ovations."

"And throw candy to the audiences."

Bonwit and Julia Gillian had once

been to a musical concert where just such a candy-throwing event had taken place, and they remembered it with great fondness.

How fun it would be when Bonwit and Julia Gillian were world-famous jazz musicians. Paris, Rome, Madrid: The world would be their oyster. Julia Gillian's downstairs neighbor, Enzo, was fond of that saying, and Julia Gillian had taken a shine to it as well. Bonwit must be thinking along the same lines, because he turned to Julia Gillian with the kind of smile she only saw once in a while on his face, a dreamy smile that always made her happy.

"Trumpet lessons," he said.

"Trumpet lessons," she agreed.

That was all they needed to say, because they understood each other so well. Julia Gillian and Bonwit had much in common. Both liked doing art projects, both liked eating cookies, both enjoyed long walks, and both were only children. While some people felt it must be lonely being an only child, both Julia Gillian and Bonwit loved it. They liked the calm happiness of their homes and the fact that they never had to share their belongings or their parents. Between themselves, they referred to their longtime friendship as The One and Onlys Club.

Now here was Mr. Mixler, standing outside the music room door, greeting the students passing by. He tended to speak in exclamation marks.

"Greetings, musicians!" said Mr. Mixler, waving his baton at Julia Gillian and Bonwit. "Welcome to the wonderful world of the trumpet!"

At each year's Welcome to Lake Harriet Elementary School Open House, Mr. Mixler described himself as a man who lived and breathed music, and it did seem to be true. Mr. Mixler played the piano on the first-floor landing each morning as the school doors opened and the students poured in. He played the piano each afternoon as the students poured out. He hummed or whistled or sang as he walked down the halls. He was known for his music-themed clothes. And he was especially known for his ever-present baton, which accompanied his every word so expressively that it was known as the Mixler baton.

Today, Mr. Mixler was wearing his famous musical-note pants, which were white, with a pattern of black notes scattered happily over the legs. He stood before the six trumpet students, nodding and smiling.

"What a lucky time of life this is for you," he said. "A lucky, lucky time of life."

He tapped the Mixler baton against an extra-large note on his pants.

"And why is that? Because you now have the tremendous

privilege of studying a musical instrument. Your lives will be forever richer because of this opportunity."

Julia Gillian looked at Bonwit and smiled. Bonwit opened his eyes wide, which was something he did when he was especially happy. As kindergartners, they had gazed up at the fifth-graders, so tall and confident, nonchalantly carrying their musical instruments back and forth from the music room.

"Tuba?" Julia Gillian would say, guessing by the size and shape of the instrument case.

"French horn," Bonwit would say, and then it would be his turn to guess.

"Flute?"

"Piccolo."

"Violin?"

"Cello."

And so it went, back when they were kindergartners. How exciting, thought Julia Gillian, finally to be old enough to sit in the music room holding an actual musical instrument on her lap.

"This week," said Mr. Mixler, "we will be learning about our trumpets. We will study the valves and we will learn how to clean a trumpet after it has been played. And we will practice buzzing into our mouthpieces until proper embouchure has been achieved."

Bonwit and Julia Gillian looked at each other. Buzzing sounded like fun. Neither of them knew what the word *embouchure* meant, but it sounded important.

"*Embouchure* is a French word," said Mr. Mixler, "which refers to proper mouth placement on the instrument."

French? This meant that *embouchure* was Julia Gillian's first foreign-language word.

"Next week, we will begin playing the trumpet, and we will learn our very first trumpet piece, 'Song of My Soul.'"

It was hard to believe that just one week from now, they would be playing an actual song. Secretly, Julia Gillian was glad that they would be learning "Song of My Soul" before "Let's Go, Band!" as it seemed a much better fit with her and Bonwit's preference for jazz. She pictured a stage in Paris, twenty years from now, when she and Bonwit were world-famous traveling jazz musicians with perfect embouchure.

"May I tell you a secret?" said Mr. Mixler.

The six students nodded. Certainly, Mr. Mixler could tell them a secret. They would be happy to hear a secret from Mr. Mixler, one of Lake Harriet's all-time favorite teachers. They sat on chairs in a semicircle, their trumpets in cases on their laps, Mr. Mixler standing before them.

"The trumpet," said Mr. Mixler, "is my personal favorite instrument."

He nodded slowly and looked at each of them in turn.

"As a music teacher, I respect all instruments. And yet the trumpet is where I have found the greatest joy."

He closed his eyes and nodded. The Mixler baton did a small wavery dance in the air.

"Where is the joy, students?" said Mr. Mixler. "That is the question I always ask myself, and it is a good question for you to ask yourselves, too."

He opened his eyes.

"Where is the joy?" he repeated. "In my life, the joy is in music. May it be so in yours, too."

Listening to Mr. Mixler, Julia Gillian felt a surge of happiness. She was a lucky person, she thought, to be here at Lake Harriet, studying the instrument she had always wanted to study, with the famous Mr. Mixler.

"Very well, then," said Mr. Mixler. "Let the wild trumpetus begin!"

CHAPTER TWO

Meet the Dumpling Man

Next day at lunch, Julia Gillian and Bonwit sat at their usual table with Cerise and Lathrop. Lathrop, who had just gotten braces, was looking with envy at the next table, where a fourth-grade boy was blowing an enormous bubble. Lathrop loved gum, but he wasn't supposed to chew any until his braces were off. Cerise was peeling back the cellophane covering her raspberry applesauce. She was a longtime purchaser of Lake Harriet hot lunch, while Julia Gillian and Bonwit had always brought their lunches from home.

Since kindergarten, Bonwit had been known both for his interesting lunches, usually made by his father,

and his lunch bag faces, drawn with Magic Marker on his brown paper lunch bag by his mother. The faces were always interesting because Bonwit's mother was an artist.

"I wish my mother had time for lunch bag faces," said Cerise. "You guys are so lucky to be only children."

Cerise had four brothers and sisters, which meant, according to Cerise, that every child in the family was doomed to hot lunch from first grade on. Lathrop also bought hot lunch, but Lathrop was known as a human garbage can who had never met a lunch he didn't like. Of course, his new braces were now limiting the foods he could eat.

"My parents can't even keep us straight," said Cerise. "Half the time they call us by one another's names."

She shook her head sadly and picked at her raspberry applesauce with her spork.

"Being an only child is great," agreed Julia Gillian. "Right, Bonwit?"

Bonwit said nothing. He was intent on laying out each item of his lunch on his paper napkin.

"Think of how long your mother's been decorating your lunch bags," said Julia Gillian. "She might have set a record by now."

"Maybe," said Bonwit.

"You can always tell what mood she's in by the expression on the face," said Lathrop.

Bonwit unwrapped his sandwich, which appeared to be tuna with thinly sliced pickle on honey whole wheat bread from the Great Harvest Bread Bakery. Julia Gillian peered at the half-sandwich Bonwit now held in his hand. Did it contain a thin layer of crushed potato chips between the tuna and the bread? It did. That meant that Bonwit's mother had made his sandwich today. Bonwit's father did not believe in potato chips on bread. Not even the thinnest of layers.

Not even if Bonwit liked potato chips on his tuna, which he did.

"Especially when they're faces of negativity," added Julia Gillian.

This was true. Over the years, Bonwit's mother had become known for the frowns, bared teeth, stuck-out tongues, tears of sorrow, and squinched eyes of rage that she sometimes drew on Bonwit's lunch bags. Bonwit had assured Julia Gillian that art did not necessarily reflect the personality of the artist, and she knew from personal experience that his mother was a very nice person. Not to mention an excellent baker of cookies, which Julia Gillian had often enjoyed while visiting Bonwit.

Bonwit took a bite of his tuna sandwich. There was the faintest crunch as he chewed. That was from the thin layer of potato chips. She reached out and turned his lunch bag around so that she could see the face of the day, but the bag was just an ordinary brown paper bag.

"Where's your face of the day?"

"There isn't one."

"Why not?"

"Because," said Bonwit, "I make my own lunches now."

He revolved his lunch bag so that both Julia Gillian and Cerise could view all four sides. The bag was indeed faceless.

"You make your own lunches?" said Julia Gillian.

"Since when?"

"Since today."

This was a surprise to Julia Gillian, whose parents had always made her lunches for her. She liked to sit at the breakfast table and watch her mother wash an apple for her lunch. She liked the way her father used the cheese slicer to slice the cheese for her sandwiches. She preferred her cheese sliced extremely thin, and her father was expert in the Art of Thinly Sliced Cheese.

She also liked the notes that her parents left for her in her lunch bags. The notes were very small — no bigger than a typical fortune from a fortune cookie — and sometimes all they said was *xoxoxo*, which meant hugs and kisses. Julia Gillian had received one in her lunch bag every day of her school life. She had saved every one and kept most of them in a Hush Puppies shoe box next to the larger box that contained her collection of homemade masks. One of Julia Gillian's many talents was the Art of Papier-Mâché Mask Making. No one but she knew that some of her tiny lunch notes were pasted into the interior of her favorite mask, which was a fierce raccoon mask. They were there to give her extra courage when she needed it.

But Bonwit, her best friend, made his own lunches now. Did this mean that Julia Gillian was falling behind? *With age comes greater responsibility*, Ms. Schultz was fond of saying, and perhaps making your own lunch was one way to demonstrate greater responsibility.

"Do your parents still make your lunches?" said Bonwit.

He was watching her closely from behind his tuna–potato chip sandwich.

"Oh no," said Julia Gillian. "I make them myself."

She heard herself saying these words in a nonchalant tone of voice. The minute they were said, she wanted to grab them back — after all, they were not true — but it was too late. Bonwit was nodding.

"It's kind of babyish to have your parents make your lunch," he said.

"Indeed it is," said Julia Gillian automatically.

Indeed it is was another of her favorite phrases. But she could not enjoy the way it sounded, because she was suddenly in a pickle. Julia Gillian had never before told a lie to her best friend, and this one had just popped out of her mouth. Now she sat next to him, unable to open her lunch bag. What if he should see her tiny folded note? How would she be able to eat her lunch?

Just then, Lathrop came to her rescue.

"How did trumpet lessons go yesterday?" he asked.

"Great," said Julia Gillian, in relief.

"Great," said Bonwit.

"Really?" said Cerise.

"Really," said Bonwit. "Mr. Mixler taught us how to put our trumpets together and take them apart."

"Did you play them?"

"Not yet. It was an introductory day. He talked about correct embouchure and correct posture. I love the trumpet. It's my personal favorite instrument."

This was a long speech for Bonwit, who was in general a quiet person.

"How do you know for sure, then, if you haven't even played the thing yet?" said Cerise.

It was a reasonable question, and Bonwit took all questions seriously. He paused to consider.

"I guess I don't know for absolute sure," he said. "But still, I'm pretty sure."

Cerise rolled her eyes. Julia Gillian had, in fact, played both the recorder and the triangle before, so she had a bit more experience than Bonwit. That she had played the recorder and the triangle in her bedroom, with only Bigfoot as witness, did not change that fact. She was about to ask Cerise if she knew what *embouchure* was, so she could explain that it was a musical term meaning correct mouth position, when they were interrupted by the sharp toot of the principal's whistle. Ms. Smartt stood at the front of the lunchroom, waving her arms and tooting her whistle, something she was fond of doing.

"I have an announcement," she said. "Sad news, students. Mrs. K has broken her ankle."

All the students looked at each other in alarm. Mrs. K, the beloved Lake Harriet lunch lady, had broken her ankle? The lunchroom was immediately abuzz, and Ms. Smartt blew her whistle again.

"This is a serious injury," said Ms. Smartt, "and it means that Mrs. K will need to recuperate at home for quite some time."

Oh dear. This was terrible news. Poor Mrs. K. Julia Gillian felt a sudden sharp longing for her and her dog-head cane. Mrs. K was always smiling, and she knew every child's name.

"Until such time as Mrs. K can return," said Ms. Smartt, "we will have an interim lunch monitor."

An interim lunch monitor? Julia Gillian did not know what *interim* meant, but it didn't sound good.

"And here he is," said Ms. Smartt, tooting her whistle at a red-haired man standing to her left. "Please give a warm Lake Harriet welcome to Mr. Wintz."

Julia Gillian and Bonwit were too stunned to do anything but stare at each other. This was happening too fast. Overnight they had lost their beloved Mrs. K,

to be replaced by a lunch *man*? They observed the red-haired lunch man in silence. He was carrying a plastic bag of baby carrots. He wore a white T-shirt with a crudely drawn Chinese pot sticker on the chest. A pen was wedged above his left ear, and a purple fanny pack was strapped around his hips. From where she sat, Julia Gillian could just make out the words *Dumpling Man* around the pot sticker.

Mrs. K did not have red hair, and Julia Gillian had never seen her carrying a bag of baby carrots. Also, Mrs. K would never wear a Dumpling Man T-shirt. Ms. Smartt blew her principal's whistle again, two short toots this time, which meant that the students could return to what they were doing.

CHAPTER THREE

The Confiscation of Cookies

Julia Gillian and Bonwit looked at each other in consternation — a lunch man? Wearing a Dumpling Man T-shirt and crunching baby carrots? She didn't know what to think. A tiny inscription gouged into the wooden tabletop caught her eye, and she leaned close to read it.

Vince Knows All.

Who was Vince? Julia Gillian was quite sure that no current student at Lake Harriet was named Vince. Vince struck her as a name from a former generation, or perhaps a former century. Julia Gillian peered at the inscription again. It had been dug into the wooden tabletop with a pen. Perhaps a quill pen. Julia Gillian pictured a small

VINCE KNOWS ALL

boy in knickers and a cap, secretly

scratching his name into the tabletop

for all eternity.

Hello, Vince, she beamed telepathically

to Vince, whoever he might be, across time

and space. It was possible that, had they

lived a hundred years ago, she and Bonwit might have

been friends with this Vince.

Bonwit finished his tuna–potato chip sandwich and

pulled a four-pack of Oreos out of his lunch bag.

"Oreos?" said Julia Gillian. "Why are you, of all people, bringing Oreos?"

They were her favorite store-bought cookie, but it was odd to see them in Bonwit's lunch. His mother was an excellent baker, and homemade cookies were her specialty. Her Triple-Chip Supremes were famous throughout the fifth grade.

"Want one?" said Bonwit.

He wasn't answering her question, and this, too, was odd.

"Indeed I do," said Julia Gillian. "Thank you very much, Bonwit."

It was not like Julia Gillian and Bonwit to be so polite with each other, and Bonwit gave her a quizzical look. This lunch hour had been full of surprises. First Julia Gillian had told Bonwit that she now made her own lunches, which was a lie, and now she was being oddly polite, not to mention that Mrs. K had been replaced by a man wearing a dumpling T-shirt.

"You're very welcome, Julia Gillian," said Bonwit, which made Julia Gillian laugh.

Bonwit opened his four-pack and handed an Oreo to Julia Gillian.

"Excuse me," a voice said. "What are you doing?"

Bonwit, Cerise, Lathrop, and Julia Gillian turned to behold the lunch man standing behind them. Instinctively, Julia Gillian hid her right hand, which was holding the Oreo Bonwit had just given her, under the table.

"Watch out," said Lathrop. "It's the Dumpling Man."

This was bold, even for Lathrop, and Julia Gillian knew from the look on his face that he had blurted out the words from sheer surprise. The lunch man frowned.

"My name is not the Dumpling Man," he said.

At this, Julia Gillian, Bonwit, Lathrop, and Cerise stiffened in their seats and did not dare look at each other. This was one of those times when someone said something not intended to be funny, but which was — unexpectedly — terribly funny. Julia Gillian feared that Cerise would start to laugh so hard that milk would squirt out her nose, as had happened once in second grade.

"And I'm speaking to you," said the lunch man.

The lunch man tapped Bonwit's four-pack of Oreos with his index finger.

"This is what I'm talking about."

Underneath the table, in solidarity with Bonwit, Julia Gillian clasped her hand tightly around her Oreo.

"Are you aware of the school rule about no sharing of lunches?"

Julia Gillian, Bonwit, Lathrop, and Cerise looked at each other. Could this possibly be true? They had always shared their lunches, and Mrs. K had never said a thing.

"Um," said Bonwit. "No."

"Well," said the lunch man. "Now you know. No sharing of lunches whatsoever. I'm afraid I'll have to confiscate those cookies."

All the students sat perfectly still. The entire lunchroom had heard the dreaded word: *confiscate*.

"Federal health regulations," said the lunch man. "Need I say more?"

He gave his bag of baby carrots a little shake, then extracted one and bit off half with a snap. Federal health regulations. Julia Gillian wasn't sure what that meant, but the phrase had an ominous sound. She imagined men and women in white laboratory coats, silently descending on the Lake Harriet lunchroom and making official notes on clipboards.

The lunch man popped the second half of his baby carrot into his mouth.

Crunch.

"Cookies, please."

He held out his hand, and Bonwit, like a child robot obeying directions, handed over the remaining three Oreos. The lunch man unzipped his purple fanny pack and placed the Oreos inside it. Then he took out a little notebook, withdrew his pen from above his ear, and jotted something down.

Then he rotated in a slow circle, crunching his baby carrot and surveying the lunchroom, which was perfectly still. He nodded once, in a business-like manner. Bonwit and Cerise and Julia Gillian swiveled on their bench to watch him stride to the end of their row of tables. The lunch man then made a swift about-face and marched down the next row. All the students turned to study him as he passed. Every half-row, he extracted another baby carrot.

Crunch.

"I don't like that Dumpling Man," said Cerise. "Not one bit."

Under the table, Julia Gillian was still holding the Oreo that Bonwit had given her, the fateful Oreo that had started the whole lunch-man chain of events. She could feel it beginning to crumble. She peeked at it under the table, and then she looked at Bonwit. Then, before she knew what was happening, Julia Gillian scooted her hand out from under the table and popped the entire Oreo into her mouth.

Cerise and Lathrop gasped.

Cerise's eyes widened.

Julia Gillian chewed fast.

"Julia Gillian, in my entire life, I have never seen you do anything like that," said Bonwit.

This was true. Julia Gillian was known as an exceptionally law-abiding citizen. She was the kind of girl who stayed within the parameters her parents set for her. She was the kind of girl who always carried an extra plastic bag when she walked Bigfoot, just in case. She was the kind of girl who told the truth.

But here, in the space of a single lunch period, she had lied to her best friend and broken a federal health regulation. Was this what it felt like to be someone else?

♪

All the Lake Harriet students were relieved when the final lunch bell rang and they could leave the lunchroom and the new lunch man. Poor Bonwit, who truly loved dessert, had not had even a single Oreo. And Julia Gillian had not even tasted her illegal Oreo because she'd eaten it so quickly. What a strange lunch it had been.

Julia Gillian was glad it was Friday, which was the start of the weekend. It was Bonwit and Julia Gillian's routine to spend many weekend afternoons at either of their homes, doing homework together, making art projects, or practicing their free throws. Julia Gillian hadn't been to Bonwit's house since school ended last June, because Bonwit and his parents had spent the summer in Vermont. Bonwit's father was a carpenter, and he had built an addition onto Bonwit's grandparents' house.

Julia Gillian missed Bonwit's house. Since his mother was an artist and his father a carpenter, theirs was a home full of color and wood scraps and unusual materials from which to make art projects. It was a peaceful and friendly house, and it usually smelled like cookies. How fun it would be to get back into their One and Onlys weekend routine. And now they could practice the trumpet together, which was something new to look forward to.

"Maybe we can practice our embouchure at your house tomorrow," said Julia Gillian. "Maybe your mother can bake some of her Triple-Chip Supremes."

Bonwit was moving down the hall at a good clip, but

his shoulders were hunched forward. This was a sign that he was anxious. And why wouldn't he be, thought Julia Gillian, since his Oreos had just been confiscated by Mr. Dumpling. At any rate, he did not appear to have heard her. She spoke again, a little louder this time.

"Shall we make some plans for tomorrow?"

Bonwit shook his head.

"Sunday, then?"

He shook his head again.

"Why not?"

But Bonwit just shook his head. This was strange. Was Bonwit angry because Julia Gillian had gobbled his Oreo, while the remaining three had been confiscated?

Julia Gillian decided to wait until they were walking home to ask Bonwit what was troubling him. Both of them were walkers by nature, and their parents had given them permission to walk home from Lake Harriet as long as they were in the company of each other. The walk home was long, but nice. There was only one truly bad intersection at the corner of Richfield Road and Lake Calhoun, which Julia Gillian and Bonwit referred to as the Intersection of Fear. But both were well schooled in the Art of Looking Both Ways, waiting for the little white crosswalk man, and looking both ways again before they crossed.

Once they reached the Intersection of Fear, Julia Gillian asked again about the weekend.

"Bonwit, do you want to come to my apartment tomorrow to practice our embouchure?"

This option would be fine, although in truth Julia Gillian would prefer Bonwit's house. She pictured the vase of peacock feathers, the drawer full of glues of the world, and the rows and rows of paints stored on the shelves of Bonwit's dining room, where the dining table was used not for eating but, instead, for art projects.

"That's okay," said Bonwit, which was a roundabout way of saying "No."

Julia Gillian took a deep breath.

"Are you angry that I ate one of your Oreos and the lunch man confiscated your others?"

"No."

"Why don't you want me to come over tomorrow, then?"

She felt a bit odd, asking again like this, but Bonwit *was* her best friend. He trudged along through the autumn leaves drifting over the sidewalk. Red and gold and orange and brown — all the colors made Julia Gillian think again about all the paints at Bonwit's house.

"My mother has a cold," said Bonwit.

"Oh."

Well, at least there was a good reason. Or a semi-good reason. They trudged in silence along the narrow sidewalk by Lakewood Cemetery. Julia Gillian ran her hand along the black iron fence. Bonwit was bowed under the weight of his backpack. They arrived at the corner of 36th and Dupont. He turned right, and she turned left.

"Bye," said Julia Gillian.

"See you Monday," said Bonwit.

A cold was one of those illnesses, thought Julia Gillian, that didn't have to make a difference in terms of a best friend coming over on a Saturday. Especially when it came to Bonwit's mother, who was a very active person and not the sort to let a cold stand in her way. A cold could also be used as an excuse. Was Bonwit using his mother's cold as an excuse? Did he actually not want Julia Gillian to come to his house? Julia Gillian had never in her life considered a possibility like this with her best friend.

CHAPTER FOUR
Time to Visit Enzo

And there you have it, said Julia Gillian silently to Bigfoot.

He looked up from his long magenta pillow, where he had been napping with his front leg tucked protectively over his skinny brown bat, and thumped his tail twice. Julia Gillian's parents were still at their own schools, and she had just finished telling him about her confusing day. She was not in the mood to hear her own voice, talking aloud to Bigfoot, so she had beamed the story to him telepathically. She and her dog were skilled at the Art of Telepathy.

I don't like keeping a secret from Bonwit. It doesn't feel right.

Also, this wasn't just keeping a secret. It was a lie, that she made her own lunches, when she did no such thing. Why? Because she didn't want to seem like a baby, that was why. And then, by eating the Oreo, she had blatantly broken a school rule. Had she somehow turned into a different person — a lying, rule-breaking sort of person — over the summer?

"And I don't like thinking that Bonwit might not want me to come over to his house anymore."

Bigfoot gazed at her and tilted his head as much as he could, given that he was lying down. Bigfoot was an agreeable dog, and he tended to thump his tail in response to anything she said. Julia Gillian looked at the fierce raccoon mask hanging on her bedpost. She turned it over so that she could read the lunch notes she had

pasted onto the back.

Courage, she thought.

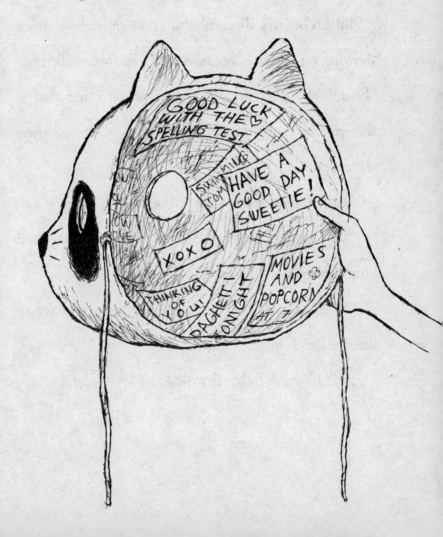

"Hello," said Julia Gillian's father, poking his head around her open door. "How was your day, Daughter?"

Julia Gillian's discombobulation must have been showing on her face, because her father only called her "Daughter" when he wanted to reassure her that if she were in need, she could call on him. It was their secret code.

"Father, have you ever heard of a lunch man?"

"I have not, Daughter. Back in my day we only had lunch ladies."

"Well, Mrs. K broke her ankle. And now we have an interim lunch man."

Julia Gillian's father frowned.

"I'm sorry, honey," he said. "I know how much you like Mrs. K."

A wave of missing Mrs. K came sweeping through Julia Gillian. She tried to hide it from her father. It seemed childish to be missing her former lunch lady so much.

"Is there anything else, Daughter?"

"Yes. I don't want any more notes in my lunch," said Julia Gillian.

This was completely untrue, but Julia Gillian heard herself saying the words anyway. Her father tilted his head and looked at her.

"I'm too old for them," she said. "I'm ten now."

Her father nodded slowly.

"As you wish, Daughter," he said.

Julia Gillian suddenly wanted to take back her words. She was only ten, after all, and not ready to give up her tiny folded lunch notes. But then she thought of Bonwit, who made his own lunches now, and she kept quiet.

KNOCK. KNOCK. KNOCK.

KnockKnockKnock.

Knock. Knock. Knock.

This was Julia Gillian's secret knocking code for Enzo and Zap's apartment door, which was located one floor below the Gillians'.

"Come on in, Noodlie!" came Enzo's voice from within.

Julia Gillian opened
the door with the
key that she kept
on a string around her neck, along with her
own key. Noodlie was Enzo's pet name for
Julia Gillian, and hearing it made Julia
Gillian feel safe and loved. Enzo had been
Julia Gillian's neighbor for years, and she
looked after her when her parents had to be
gone for more than an hour.

"Hey, JG," came a deep voice from
within the apartment.

Julia Gillian couldn't see him, but
she knew that Zap must be there,
because no one but Zap called

Julia Gillian "JG." Zap was a student at the Dunwoody Culinary Institute, where he was studying to be the best chef in the history of the world. Enzo was a student at Metropolitan State University, where she didn't know exactly what she most wanted to study. She was enjoying herself and expanding her mind, though, and Enzo said that was the most important thing.

"Zap is an extraordinary cook," Julia Gillian's father had said.

"And at such a young age," Julia Gillian's mother had said.

Now Julia Gillian removed her flip-flops and walked into Zap and Enzo's apartment. Zap saluted Bigfoot and then beckoned him closer.

"JG," he sang in a low opera-singer sort of voice. "JG, JG, JG, JG."

His voice climbed the scale with each intonation of JG. Julia Gillian smiled at Zap. He, along with Enzo, was one of her favorite people. Maybe things were not so troubling after all.

"Hello, my Bigfoot," said Zap. "How are you, my canine friend?"

Next to her, Bigfoot's body trembled. He loved Zap so much that it was almost hard for him to be in his presence. Julia Gillian was not jealous of Zap, because she knew that she came first in Bigfoot's heart and soul.

"Go on and say hi to him," Julia Gillian encouraged Bigfoot.

Bigfoot wagged his tail so strongly that Julia Gillian was nearly knocked sideways. He trotted over to Zap, who buried his hands in the fur behind Bigfoot's ears. He liked to be scratched in

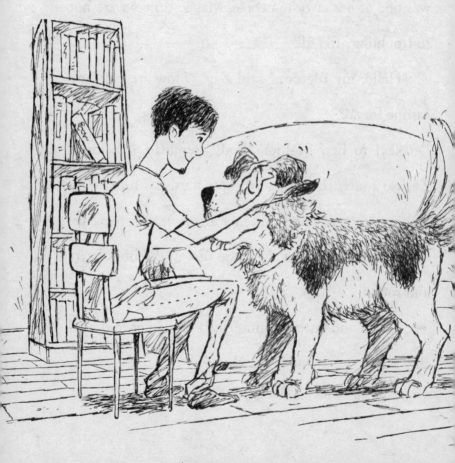

that particular place, and Zap liked to make him happy.

"How was your day, Noodlie?" said Enzo.

Enzo was sitting cross-legged in her brown velvet

chair, studying. She was determined to maintain a 4.0 GPA at Metropolitan State University. Julia Gillian wasn't exactly sure what that meant, but she knew it meant that Enzo studied a great deal. Enzo loved to study, however, and she loved to read, especially *The Collected Works of William Shakespeare*. Shakespeare was her literary hero. For some reason, this made Julia Gillian feel a bit lonely. She didn't mind studying, but she didn't like to read.

"Not good," said Julia Gillian.

Enzo peered up at Julia Gillian from her brown velvet chair.

"Tell."

"Well, we have an interim lunch monitor," said Julia Gillian.

"What's her name?"

"*His* name is the Dumpling Man. That's what we nicknamed him, anyway. He wears a Dumpling Man T-shirt."

"Is this Dumpling Man nice?"

"No. He confiscated Bonwit's Oreos."

"Why?"

"Federal health regulation."

Julia Gillian usually didn't speak in such short sentences when she was with Enzo, and Enzo looked a bit worried.

"Noodlie?" she said. "Is anything else wrong?"

Enzo was not one to mince words, which was one of the things that Julia Gillian appreciated about her. She had known Enzo for a long time, and Enzo had always helped her solve her problems. But Julia Gillian was getting older now. She thought of Bonwit, who made his own lunches, and Cerise, whose parents were so busy that they didn't have much time for her.

It's time for me to start solving my own problems, thought Julia Gillian, *even if I don't really want to.*

"No," she said. "Everything's fine."

But that, too, was a lie. Julia Gillian was digging herself deeper and deeper.

CHAPTER FIVE

The Trail of Silence

"Dumpling alert," whispered Cerise.

Julia Gillian sat up straight. She hadn't meant to, but there was something about the lunch man that made slouching nearly impossible. Two weeks had passed since the lunch man had come to Lake Harriet Elementary, and the atmosphere in the lunch room was markedly changed.

"Lathrop, is it true that your parents got The Call?" said Cerise.

Lathrop, his mouth full of creamed corn, nodded. The lunch man had instituted a new call-the-parents policy at Lake Harriet for students who repeatedly did not eat their lunches, especially the fruits or vegetables.

Lathrop had been cited for not finishing his green beans. Cerise's parents had gotten The Call last week, after the lunch man noted that for three days in a row she had not finished her baby carrots.

Julia Gillian looked down at her own lunch. No baby carrots today, but she did have a kiwi, which was not one of her favorite fruits. No matter. She would eat it anyway, if only to avoid The Call.

"What's so great about baby carrots anyway?" said Cerise. "I hear that if you eat too many of them you'll turn orange."

The Dumpling Man turned his head from side to side, observing the children and their lunches, munching from his bag of baby carrots as he marched up and down the aisles. The fact that the lunch man was universally referred to by Lake Harriet students as the Dumpling Man made no difference; each chattering tableful of students quieted as he strode past.

It was Monday, and Julia Gillian wondered if anyone had broken a federal health regulation today. She decided to surround herself with a bubble of invisibility, so that she would be unnoticed as the Dumpling Man made his rounds. She looked down at the Vince Knows All inscription on the table. Vince had become a source of strength for her. She cupped both hands over the inscription and closed her eyes.

"I am invisible," she whispered, "invisible am I."

Cerise looked at her curiously. Today's hot lunch was Italian Dunkers, and she held a dunker aloft like a small spear, then plunged it into the tub of dunking sauce.

"What are you muttering about?"

"I'm not muttering."

"You certainly are," said Cerise, who was not one to back down.

"Well," said Julia Gillian. "If you must know, I am muttering a spell of enchantment."

"Does it have to do with the Dumpling Man?"

Julia Gillian nodded.

"Good luck," said Lathrop.

They all needed good luck when it came to the Dumpling Man, who was rounding the end of the fourth-graders' row. Now he stopped in front of one of the fourth-graders and held out his hand. She placed a miniature Heath bar in his palm, and he transferred it to the purple fanny pack.

The fourth-grader began to cry.

"What a baby," said Lathrop.

"Be quiet," said Cerise. "She's only in fourth grade."

"Still," said Lathrop.

From far away they heard the Dumpling Man's now-familiar voice reciting now-familiar words.

"There will be no sharing of lunches in the lunchroom. That is a school rule, and as long as I am the lunch man, all rules will be enforced to the best of my ability."

The Lake Harriet students made sad faces at each other. How things had changed since the days of Mrs. K.

Look at the lunch man's fanny pack, for heaven's sake. It was already bulging with confiscated food, and lunch wasn't half over. Now he was writing in his miniature notebook. Surely it was uncomfortable, walking around with both the fanny pack and the notebook weighing him down, but the lunch man didn't seem to care.

I am invisible, thought Julia Gillian, *invisible am I.*

She decided to focus on the positive, such as the fact that on Thursday, she and Bonwit would have their trumpet lesson. Last week, Mr. Mixler had promised them that they had made excellent progress on their embouchures, so they would actually play their trumpets at the next lesson. Thursday could possibly be the start of Julia Gillian and Bonwit's future as world-famous traveling jazz musicians.

This was indeed a happy thought, but Thursday was still a long way off.

She looked down at her own lunch. Today her mother had made her a peanut butter and jelly roll-up, which was one of her favorite sandwiches. Next to her, Bonwit took a bite of his own sandwich, which was cream cheese and jelly on soft white bread. Julia Gillian knew how difficult it was to spread cream cheese on bread like that; the bread tended to crumble and break under the pressure of the knife. Now that Bonwit was making his own lunches, how had he managed?

"Where's your lunch bag note?" Bonwit said.

He was looking at her curiously. How long had she been sitting at the lunch table, gazing down at her uneaten peanut butter and jelly roll-up? The lunch man was at the far end of the lunch room now. He had left a trail of silence in his wake. Only when he was well past each table did subdued chatter start up again.

"I don't have one," said Julia Gillian. "I make my own lunches now. Remember?"

She put her uneaten roll-up back into her lunch bag and then crumpled up the bag in a carefree way, as if she were a carefree girl who did not care that she didn't get tiny lunch notes anymore. She looked at Bonwit, eating the face-free lunch that he had made for himself. She looked at Cerise, who was finishing the chocolate milk that she selected every day as her hot lunch beverage option.

She looked at Lathrop, who was spooning up the last of his applesauce. Every day he made sure to tell them that soft foods, like vanilla pudding and apple-sauce, were good for you. Now he was putting a fresh elastic band on his new braces. Although he com-plained about them frequently, Julia Gillian could tell that Lathrop was secretly proud of being the first of the four to get braces. It was a sad day when Lathrop Fallon had surpassed Julia Gillian in growth and maturity.

None of them had any idea how much Julia Gillian missed her lunch notes.

She traced the Vince Knows All inscription with her index finger, as was her habit each lunch day, and telepathically beamed him good wishes.

After school, Julia Gillian and Bonwit walked home together. Next to her, Bonwit was quiet. She thought ahead to the coming weekend.

"Does your mother still have a cold?" she said.

Bonwit nodded.

"Do you think it'll be gone by Saturday?"

Bonwit shook his head.

"Boy, that's a bad cold, isn't it?" said Julia Gillian.

She didn't like the sound of her own voice, which sounded like Cerise at her most sarcastic. But Bonwit didn't look up.

"It's all the Dumpling Man's fault," she said suddenly. "Don't you think?"

"What's all the Dumpling Man's fault?"

"This," said Julia Gillian, spreading her arms wide.

"This what?"

Good question. Until recently, Bonwit would have known what she meant, even if Julia Gillian couldn't put it into words. But that was before the lunch man, and the Oreo, and the lie, and the ending of the lunch notes.

"This no sharing of lunches," she tried to explain. "This enforcing of school rules. This making your own lunch with no Magic Marker faces. Everything's changed since the Dumpling Man arrived."

Now Bonwit looked up. Julia Gillian had not intended to bring up the making of his own lunch, but she had.

"You make your own lunch, too, you know," said Bonwit.

"I know."

This was Julia Gillian's first experience with lying, and she wasn't sure if "I know" counted as another lie or a continuation of the original one. She had a sense of the days and weeks to come, one Julia Gillian–Bonwit walk home blurring into another, backpacks slumping off their shoulders, feet trudging along, barely speaking. Would the lunchroom ever again be the happy place it had once been? Would Bonwit's mother have a cold for the rest of her life? Would Julia Gillian ever sit at Bonwit's dining room table again surrounded with interesting art materials and fresh-baked cookies?

Where was the joy?

CHAPTER SIX

Song of My Soul

"Trumpeters, please raise your trumpets," said Mr. Mixler.

The students had just spent the past hour buzzing their trumpets and practicing the fingering for "Song of My Soul," which had three distinct parts. The fingering was not easy, especially in the tricky ending. Julia Gillian felt fairly sure of herself in the smooth middle section, and the beginning was not too bad, but that ending did give her pause. Now Bonwit raised his trumpet and smiled at Julia Gillian, which she found encouraging.

"Place your trumpet in playing position. Pay particular attention to your embouchure."

Julia Gillian placed her trumpet on her mouth and paid particular attention to her embouchure. Next to her, Bonwit did the same. Mr. Mixler was wearing his famous musical note shirt. He was a true musician, thought Julia Gillian.

"Remember, my dear students, to look for the joy."

The Mixler baton swept through the air.

"And, play!"

The room erupted in noise. Trumpet squawks and trumpet bleats and trumpet burps filled the air of the music room. Julia Gillian wondered what sort of sound she herself was making on her trumpet. With six students all playing at once, it was difficult to discern who was making which noise. One clear high note floated above all the others. *Maybe that's me*, thought Julia Gillian, until she saw that it was Mr. Mixler, playing his own trumpet.

"Trumpets down," called Mr. Mixler.

The students put their trumpets down and turned to each other. Everyone was smiling and laughing. It did seem amazing to Julia Gillian that by their third lesson, they had been able to produce such a variety of noise. Maybe that was because they had worked so hard on their embouchures.

"That sounded like joy to me," said Mr. Mixler, nodding. "Let's try again, this time one at a time. Mr. Keller, will you begin? Let's hear the first note of 'Song of My Soul.'"

Bonwit raised his trumpet to his lips, took a deep breath, and blew. A squawk louder than Julia Gillian ever would have thought Bonwit capable came out of his trumpet. She looked at her friend in amazement. His eyes were wide, his cheeks were red, and the squawk kept coming until, abruptly, Bonwit's breath ended. He lowered the trumpet to his lap. *Good job*, Julia Gillian beamed telepathically to Bonwit, and he turned to her again and smiled.

Next up was Sam Harris, whose trumpet sounded as if it was bleating.

Then came Mia Martin, who, after some initial difficulty, managed to make what sounded like a burp.

Tanisha Duckworth sounded a very loud high note.

Doua Lee's trumpet reminded Julia Gillian of a foghorn; it was that loud and deep. She had the urge to cover her ears, but she resisted, since she didn't want to hurt Doua's feelings.

Now it was Julia Gillian's turn. She was nervous, but excited. She raised her trumpet to her lips and took a deep breath, preparing to blow, when a loud bell rang throughout the school. For a moment Julia Gillian was confused, thinking that somehow she herself had produced such a loud sound, but then realized it was the fire alarm.

Fire drills were taken very seriously at Lake Harriet Elementary, and Mr. Mixler immediately waved his baton in the air.

"Trumpets down," he said. "Students out."

And Julia Gillian put her trumpet down and filed out of the music room in an orderly fashion. Bonwit, next to her, gave her a sympathetic look.

"I'm sorry you didn't get to play," he said above the sound of the fire alarm.

Julia Gillian was sorry, too. She had been looking forward to hearing whatever interesting sound her own trumpet produced. But fire drills were a necessity, and she tried to be grown up about it.

"Next time," she said, and together she and Bonwit filed out of the school building and stood in an orderly fashion. Julia Gillian spotted the lunch man's red hair far down the sidewalk. He was standing with the third-graders, who looked especially small and defenseless next to his military posture. Poor little things. She squinted in order to see better. Even outside, at a fire drill, the Dumpling Man was munching on baby carrots.

♪

On their long walk home, Julia Gillian resisted asking
Bonwit about the weekend. *If he wants you to come
over, he'll ask*, she told herself. But he did not ask, and
her fears returned. Was it possible that, after so many
years of being an all-the-time best friend, Bonwit now
wanted to be a school-only friend? Such things did
happen.

"I don't want to be school-only friends with Bonwit,"
she said out loud to Bigfoot when she got home. "That's
the problem."

Bigfoot was a good listener, and now he thumped his
tail twice on the floor. It was good to be able to tell her
dog about her worries over Bonwit. But those worries
were only part of the problem. For a moment, Julia

Gillian pictured her list of accomplishments in the notebook that she kept under her mattress. She had always been proud of her accomplishments, and she had listed each one with happiness. Now she imagined adding "Skilled at the Art of Lying" to the list, and a sad shiver went through her.

Bonwit made his own lunches now, but this didn't seem to bother him. Cerise's parents couldn't keep their five children straight, and while this did bother Cerise, she was philosophical about it. Lathrop, with his new braces, was ahead of everyone else in the orthodontia department.

"My friends are growing up faster than me, Bigfoot," said Julia Gillian. "Even Bonwit. What should I do?"

Bigfoot dropped his head as if he, too, had no idea

how to solve Julia Gillian's problems. They were true friends, and true friends needed to look out for each other. *True friends*, beamed Julia Gillian telepathically to Bonwit, on the off chance that he would receive her telepathic message and invite her over the next day.

Bigfoot pawed his stuffed bat. How he loved the bat, which Julia Gillian had inadvertently won for him in the Bryant Hardware claw machine. She had been trying to win a meerkat for herself, but she had won a brown bat for Bigfoot instead. Her unhappiness at not winning the meerkat had diminished when she saw how happy the bat made him. That was another thing about being true friends. You celebrated each other's happiness. *True friends*, she beamed again to Bonwit.

Julia Gillian took her fierce raccoon mask down

from the bedpost. She tied the shoestrings behind her head and looked at Bigfoot. He thumped his tail approvingly. Julia Gillian did feel better with her raccoon mask on, especially with all the tiny pasted-in lunch notes right next to her nose. Even though she couldn't see them, she knew they were there.

CHAPTER SEVEN

And Now I Will Play the Trumpet

The fierce raccoon mask and its tiny hidden lunch notes had given her courage, and Julia Gillian felt better. Her parents were making dinner in the kitchen, and she decided to prepare a surprise for them. What would the surprise be? Their one and only daughter, performing the trumpet in front of them for the very first time.

"What do you say, Bigfoot?" she said. "Are you in the mood for a little wild trumpetus?"

Bigfoot lay on his long magenta pillow, bat tucked under his forepaw, watching Julia Gillian as, with great care, she removed her trumpet from its case. She didn't want to be responsible for causing even minor harm to a school instrument.

"Are you ready, Bigfoot?"

Bigfoot was now sitting up, his bat dangling from his mouth. Julia Gillian sensed his curiosity. Goodness knows she herself was curious. She had missed out on hearing herself play the trumpet for the first time, due to the Lake Harriet fire drill, but now it was her turn. She was glad that her dog would be the first to witness her playing.

"I will now raise my trumpet," said Julia Gillian to Bigfoot.

She raised her trumpet.

"I will now pay attention to the correct embouchure."

She paid attention to the correct embouchure.

"I will breathe from my diaphragm."

Mr. Mixler had explained that breathing from your diaphragm meant breathing from the bottom of your rib cage. Breathing from her diaphragm was not an easy task, but Julia Gillian did her best.

"And now, Dog of My Dreams, I will play."

When Julia Gillian was particularly happy, she sometimes called Bigfoot "Dog of My Dreams." He looked up at her and tilted his head, and she felt a wave of love for him. She pursed her lips and blew.

———————

Nothing.

Bigfoot tilted his head in the other direction and

gazed at her with interest. Julia Gillian decided to start over.

"And now, Dog of My Dreams, I will play."

She pursed her lips and blew again.

——————————

Nothing.

Julia Gillian sat on her bed for quite some time, her trumpet next to her. Could it be that her instrument was defective? No. Mr. Mixler had borrowed her trumpet the very first day of class in order to demonstrate "Song of My Soul" on it. She had been able to buzz into her mouthpiece like everyone else. What could the problem be?

"Come on, Bigfoot," said Julia Gillian. "Let's go see Enzo. She'll know what to do."

♪

KNOCK. KNOCK. KNOCK.

KnockKnockKnock.

Knock. Knock. Knock.

"Is that my Noodlie?" called Enzo from within.

Julia Gillian could hear Enzo walking toward the door. *Thunk. Thunk. Thunk.* That meant that she was wearing her platform heels, which made a satisfying, definitive sound with every step. Enzo had recently begun wearing platform heels so that she could experience what it was like

to be a tall person. She had three pairs, all of which she had bought at Value Village: jeweled platform sandals, lace-up platform boots, and platform sneakers in an interesting shade of dark red.

Now Julia Gillian heard the *click, snick* of the door being unlocked. She could, of course, have unlocked the door herself with her key, but sometimes it was nice to be welcomed inside by Enzo herself.

Enzo flung open the door. She was wearing her lace-up platform boots today. She surveyed Julia Gillian, who was carrying her trumpet, and Bigfoot, whose tail wagged rapidly at the sight of Enzo.

"Come in, Noodlie," said Enzo. "Sit in the indoor reading hammock."

Enzo always seemed to know when Julia Gillian had something on her mind. Now she *thunk*ed over to her brown velvet chair, which had been a gift from Zap, and sat down with both platform heels on the floor. Julia Gillian seated herself in Enzo's indoor reading hammock, which was a place of honor. How Julia Gillian longed to have an indoor hammock in her own apartment, but for reasons she did not understand, her parents didn't think it was a good idea.

"What's up, Noodlie?" said Enzo.

Now that she was here, Julia Gillian suddenly felt shy. She had talked about the trumpet for years, and Enzo knew how much she had looked forward to playing it. She had even described her dream of being half of a traveling jazz trumpet duo, and now she couldn't even make a single sound. It was embarrassing.

"How are your trumpet lessons going?" said Enzo.

Julia Gillian's stomach lurched. Was Enzo psychic? Could she read her mind? She felt the urge to try her invisibility enchantment, but it was far too late for that. She had been the one to seek out Enzo, after all.

"Great," said Julia Gillian. "I can already play 'Song of My Soul.'"

"It's only your third week and you're already playing a song?"

The hammock ropes were digging into Julia Gillian's legs, right through her jeans. Julia Gillian had always been able to talk to Enzo about what was on her mind, but now she felt a bit hesitant. Enzo was nineteen, so she counted as an adult. Ten years old was time to stop depending so much on adults, wasn't it? Look at Bonwit and Cerise — making his own lunch didn't seem to bother Bonwit at all, and with such a big family, Cerise had been independent for years.

"Yes," said Julia Gillian. "Mr. Mixler says we're the most advanced trumpet students he's ever taught."

Below Julia Gillian, Bigfoot sighed. He stretched his front legs straight out and buried his head in them. It was as if he knew that she was telling another lie.

"Well," said Enzo. "I'm impressed. Three weeks into lessons, and already playing a song."

" 'Song of My Soul,' " corrected Julia Gillian.

For some reason, it seemed important that Enzo know the exact name of the song that Julia Gillian knew how to play on her trumpet. Even though she didn't know how to play it on her trumpet. Even though she couldn't play anything at all on her trumpet. Even though she couldn't make a single sound.

CHAPTER EIGHT

The Sound of Nothing

That weekend, and every day after school the next week, Julia Gillian practiced her trumpet, although she wasn't sure that what she was doing could be called practice. She did what she could: She practiced her embouchure, she tried to breathe from her diaphragm, she practiced her fingering, she studied the treble clef and the bass clef, and she blew as hard as she could. But still, music was about sound. There seemed to be no arguing with that fact.

Could Julia Gillian be failing at the Art of the Trumpet?

Sitting on her bed, her instrument on her lap, and Bigfoot and his skinny brown bat lying on their long magenta pillow, Julia Gillian considered this question. She was a girl of many accomplishments, all of which she had listed in her notebook of accomplishments underneath her mattress, the very mattress upon which she was now sitting.

* SKILLED AT THE ART OF CHOPSTICKS
* SKILLED AT THE ART OF KNOWING
* SKILLED AT THE ART OF SPREADING GUM ACROSS TOP ROW OF TEETH
* SKILLED AT THE ART OF TELEPATHIC HUMAN-DOG COMMUNICATIONS
* SKILLED AT THE ART OF PAPIER-MÂCHÉ MAKING
* SKILLED AT THE ART OF THE CLAW MACHINE
* SKILLED AT THE ART OF JUGGLING

The list was considerable, and it covered one entire side of notebook paper and half of the other side. For most of her life, Julia Gillian had looked forward to playing a musical instrument. Now, for the first time, it seemed likely that she would not be adding one of her most coveted accomplishments to the list.

"*Unskilled* at the Art of the Trumpet," said Julia Gillian out loud, to test the sound of it.

As if he sensed her distress, Bigfoot looked up and gave her his full attention. He did not turn his head away, even for a moment, to check on his brown bat.

"Did you say something, honey?"

Her mother pushed open the door to Julia Gillian's bedroom, which was shut, but not all the way, as Julia Gillian did not like her door to be entirely closed.

"No."

"Are you sure?"

"I'm sure."

"When do your father and I get to hear you play 'Song of My Soul'?" said her mother. "Because we can't wait, you know."

Julia Gillian's parents were jazz fans, and while the saxophone was their favorite jazz instrument, they, too, had long been looking forward to the day when their daughter would be a music student.

"Sometime," said Julia Gillian.

"Sometime?" said her mother.

She gave Julia Gillian a quizzical look. Julia Gillian's mother prided herself on her intuitive powers. If her mother kept a list of her own accomplishments,

then "Skilled at the Art of Intuition" would certainly be on the list.

"Is everything all right?"

"Indeed it is." A month ago, Julia Gillian might not have said, "Indeed it is." A month ago, she might have told her parents about her various problems, such as the fact that she was now a liar and a rule-breaker and probably the only trumpet student in the history of Lake Harriet Elementary who could not get even the tiniest sound out of her instrument. She might have told them that Bonwit now made his own lunches, and he liked doing so, and he didn't miss his lunch bag faces at all, but she didn't want to make her own lunches, and she missed her tiny lunch bag notes terribly, all of which meant that she was a baby and Bonwit wasn't, and the truth was that she was worried that he didn't want to be her best friend anymore. But she had decided to solve her own problems and not ask for help. She looked at her fierce raccoon mask for strength. *If Bonwit is no longer a baby*, she thought, *then neither am I.*

"Greetings, my trumpeters!" said Mr. Mixler.

Today, Mr. Mixler was wearing his musical hat, which was a green hat with white lettering that read

Happy Happy Music all along the border. Despite the musical hat, Julia Gillian could not muster any happiness.

She had been dreading this day all week. So far, Julia Gillian's failure to produce a sound had gone undetected by everyone except Bigfoot. Her parents were under the impression that she practiced her trumpet before they came home from teaching. And she had told Bonwit, when he asked, that "Song of My Soul" was coming along beautifully. How long could she maintain this pretense?

"Are we ready?" said Mr. Mixler.

Dread prickled through Julia Gillian's arms and legs. She raised her trumpet along with everyone else and placed it on her lips.

"Let's go one by one today," Mr. Mixler said. "Ms. Gillian, will you begin with the opening bars of 'Song of My Soul'?"

"Indeed I will," said Julia Gillian automatically, as if Mr. Mixler had asked her an ordinary question and she was her ordinary self, answering in her usual *Indeed I will* way.

"Remember," said Mr. Mixler, "that the opening bars are *legato* and *andante,* smooth and moderately slow. The soul is searching for the path to joy, and yet it is lost in a dark wood."

Mr. Mixler closed his eyes and nodded sadly. The Mixler baton traced a slow and wandering path through the air.

"A one, a two, a three —"

Julia Gillian suddenly felt dizzy.

"Mr. Mixler, I feel sick."

"Oh my," said Mr. Mixler.

He looked concerned. So did Bonwit, who turned to Julia Gillian and stared at her in surprise.

"Can I —"

She gestured toward the door.

"Absolutely, Ms. Gillian. Take your time."

She got up and made her way to the door, and then down the hall to the bathroom, where she washed her hands. She held them under the blower

for a long time, until they were completely dry. Then she sat on the window ledge, looking out the window onto the playground below. Trying to solve her own problems was hard. Keeping secrets from everyone was hard. In ordinary times — before fifth grade, that is — Julia Gillian would tell Enzo or her parents if something was wrong. She would certainly tell her best friend. If only Bonwit knew that she couldn't make a sound on her trumpet. But then again, Bonwit was making plenty of sounds on his trumpet. He might think less of Julia Gillian if he knew how incompetent she was.

The bell rang and it was time to return to Ms. Schultz's room. She wondered what had happened in trumpet lessons after she left. Her backpack and trumpet were still back there in Mr. Mixler's room. She would just have to get them after school.

Julia Gillian slid down from the window ledge. Then she pushed open the door of the bathroom and headed down the hall to Ms. Schultz's classroom. *Courage*, she thought. That was something that Enzo would say to her.

Julia Gillian was already back at her desk when Bonwit returned from trumpet lessons. Bonwit was not a large boy, and he was carrying Julia Gillian's backpack and trumpet in addition to his own, so he looked almost cartoon-ishly burdened. He had put her trumpet away for her in its black vinyl case. Bonwit was a methodical person, so Julia Gillian did not worry that he had been careless with her trumpet. "Are you okay?" he whispered.

Julia Gillian nodded.

"You didn't throw up, did you?"

Julia Gillian shook her head. She and Bonwit shared a horror of throwing up. Back in their

120

kindergarten days, they had gone so far as to run from the classroom if any of their classmates showed the first signs of nausea.

"Phew," said Bonwit. "I was worried."

True friends worried about each other. Julia Gillian had a sudden urge to tell Bonwit the truth about everything. But then she thought about the fact that he no longer wanted her to come to his house, and she said nothing. *Don't be a baby,* she thought. She lifted her desktop to hide her face, which felt hot.

Bonwit leaned over and pointed at the underside of her desktop.

"Look at that," he said.

Vince Rules the Universe.

First the lunchroom, now the underside of her desktop. Julia Gillian felt a sense of relief at the sight of another Vince inscription. She traced the letters with her index finger. Vince, that small boy in knickers, was reaching through time and space to comfort her.

KNOCK. KNOCK. KNOCK.

KnockKnockKnock.

Knock. Knock. Knock.

"Let yourself in, Noodlie," called Enzo from within. "I'm pretzelizing."

Julia Gillian let herself in. Enzo was doing her exercises. She was a believer in flexibility and strength, and every day she did a series of complicated exercises on the braided rag rug in their living room. Zap referred to these exercises as Enzo's pretzelization. Julia Gillian had tried to twist herself into Enzo's flexibility and strength positions, so that someday she could add "Skilled at the Art of Pretzelization" to her list of accomplishments, but so far her efforts had not worked out. She waited until Enzo, who was holding what looked like a particularly challenging pose, finished counting to ten.

"What's up, Noodle?"

Noodle was as good a nickname as Noodlie. Julia Gillian was privately relieved that, despite her odd behavior of the last few weeks, Enzo had not yet called her Poodle. Poodle was not a good nickname, and Enzo used it only when she was unhappy with Julia Gillian.

"Nothing."

"Where's Bigfoot?"

Enzo squinted at Julia Gillian, as if Bigfoot might be hiding behind her. This would not be possible, since Julia Gillian was not large and Bigfoot was a St. Bernard, but it was highly unusual for Julia Gillian to show up at Enzo's apartment without her dog.

"I haven't been home yet."

Enzo's eyes widened. She unpretzeled herself and stood up. She knew that if Julia Gillian had come straight to her apartment before going home and taking Bigfoot on his constitutional, then something must be seriously awry.

"Talk to me," said Enzo.

"I got sick at school today."

"How are you feeling now?"

Julia Gillian was silent.

"Noodlie?"

"Fine. I'm fine now."

This was not true, but what else could Julia Gillian say? That was the problem with being a liar and a hider. Once you started, you just had to keep going.

"Where were you when you got sick?"

"I was at my trumpet lesson."

Enzo frowned.

"Which is my favorite class."

Was it possible that Julia Gillian had just told Enzo that Trumpet was her favorite class? Lies kept coming out of Julia Gillian's mouth, and each one seemed to lead to a new one. "Trumpet is going *great*," she continued. "Bonwit and I are the best in the class."

Enzo narrowed her eyes in thought. She always knew when Julia Gillian was trying to hide something.

"Is that so?"

Julia Gillian nodded.

"So you're enjoying playing the trumpet?"

"Of course. Why wouldn't I?"

"Well, Noodle, this may come as a surprise to you, but not everyone in the world *does* enjoy playing the trumpet. Me, for example. You couldn't pay me to play the trumpet."

"Well, you couldn't pay me to read," said Julia Gillian.

Julia Gillian regretted saying this the minute the words left her mouth, because she had never known anyone who loved to read as much as Enzo. Books filled the brick-and-board bookshelves of Enzo and Zap's apartment.

Books and books, hundreds of books. Thousands, maybe. But Enzo did not look insulted.

"Yes, I do like to read," said Enzo. "But not everyone does. Take Zap, for example."

"Zap doesn't like to read?"

This was an interesting concept for Julia Gillian, surrounded as she usually was by book lovers, like her parents and Enzo.

"Not unless you count cookbooks."

Now Julia Gillian pictured Zap as she had often observed him in the kitchen, a cookbook propped open on a stack of dish towels by the stove. Did a cookbook count as reading? Julia Gillian was not sure.

"But everyone's supposed to like to read," said Julia

Gillian, whose parents had long been concerned about her own dislike of reading.

"So what? Not everyone does. And some people, for example, just don't like playing the trumpet."

"Well, that someone isn't me. Because I *love* playing the trumpet."

Lies, lies, and more lies. How Julia Gillian wished she could just tell Enzo the truth. How everyone else in the class was already practicing "Song of My Soul," and she couldn't make any sound beyond a mouthpiece buzz. But she had decided to solve her own problems now, and that meant not asking for help.

CHAPTER NINE

The Reign of Terror

"Guess what."

Bonwit stood beside Julia Gillian's locker, a look of grimness on his face. It reminded her of a face of negativity from back in the days of the lunch bag faces. Julia Gillian sighed inwardly. She did miss those lunch bag faces. How could Bonwit have let them go so easily? Because Bonwit was not a baby, that was how.

"What?" she said.

"Lathrop got The Call."

"The Dumpling Man call?"

Bonwit nodded.

"Was it the celery sticks?"

He nodded again.

"That is so unfair," said Julia Gillian. "Did he not even listen when Lathrop told him about the braces?"

Last week, Lathrop had been faced with cut-up celery sticks in his hot lunch. They were a forbidden food for braces-wearers, but that apparently made no difference to the lunch man. And now Lathrop's parents had gotten The Call. This was even more unfair because celery was one of the few vegetables that Lathrop actually liked to eat. Bonwit and Julia Gillian were now passing Mr. Mixler's room. He was standing outside his classroom door, tapping the Mixler baton on his thigh. Was he ever without his baton? It was as familiar a sight as Mrs. K's dog-head cane had been.

"Ms. Gillian, are you feeling better?"

"Yes, I am, Mr. Mixler. Thank you."

Mr. Mixler smiled. "Excellent. And did you manage to find time to practice your trumpet despite your illness?"

"Indeed I did."

"And how goes 'Song of My Soul,' Ms. Gillian?"

"Great. I love the trumpet. The trumpet is my favorite instrument."

Julia Gillian heard herself reciting these words as if she were reading from a script. In a way, she *was* reading from a script, because they were the same familiar trumpet words that she had been saying to her parents and Enzo for the past two weeks.

"Excellent," said Mr. Mixler. "And, Mr. Keller, how is your mother faring?"

"Good."

According to Julia Gillian's English-teacher father, Bonwit should have said "Fine," or "Well," but Mr. Mixler didn't correct him.

"Knowing your mother, she's not one to take kindly to inactivity," said Mr. Mixler.

"No."

"Not too much longer, though, right?"

"Right."

Now Julia Gillian turned to look at Bonwit. She wanted to say that all this fuss about a cold was annoying, and no excuse for not letting a best friend come visit, but that would make her sound like a whiny baby, so she resisted.

Julia Gillian reached both hands behind herself and gave her backpack a little tug to readjust its weight. Her raccoon mask was in the front compartment, protected by a layer of bubble wrap so as not to crush its fragile papier-mâché-ness. She felt the need for reassurance, and what was more reassuring than the fierce courage of her raccoon mask, with its hidden pasted-in lunch notes?

Bonwit had brought his lunch in a plastic *Star Tribune* newspaper bag today. If Bonwit's mother had made his lunch today, she would have packed it in a clean paper bag. What sort of face would she have markered onto it? Perhaps a face of negativity, which would reflect the general mood of the Lake Harriet Elementary lunchroom.

Ms. Schultz's entire class had written Get Well letters to Mrs. K. Julia Gillian had drawn a picture of Bigfoot on hers, and she had signed it *Your friend, Julia Gillian (a fellow true dog person)*. She wondered what Mrs. K was doing during her recuperation. Maybe she was knitting multicolored scarves, which was something that Julia Gillian's father liked to do.

Maybe she was making origami cranes, like the ones that Tanisha Duckworth had brought in to school for Show & Know, and which Mrs. K had admired.

YOUR FRIEND, JULIA GILLIAN (A FELLOW TRUE DOG) PERSON

Whatever Mrs. K was doing in her recuperation, that did not change what the Dumpling Man was doing in the lunchroom. As she did every day, Julia Gillian looked down at the tiny Vince Knows All inscription on the lunch table. Vince, that long-ago boy in knickers, would no doubt have felt the same about the Dumpling Man as she did.

Lathrop, who was eating tapioca pudding, used his spoon to gesture at the Dumpling Man. Cerise and Julia Gillian and Bonwit turned to watch him marching down the far aisle, just past the third-graders. The students in the Dumpling Man's wake were so quiet that the *crunch* of his baby carrot was clearly audible. When he reached the end of the row, he made his military turn and came marching back down, leaving silence and good posture in his wake.

Things had grown increasingly grim under the rule of the Dumpling Man. He had added good posture and chewing with a closed mouth to his list of rules. It was not uncommon for a student to be faced with the Dumpling Man standing before him making the sign of the zipped lip, or reprimanding her for not sitting up straight.

"Everything is ruined," said Cerise. "Everything!"

Cerise was prone to exaggeration, but in this case Bonwit and Julia Gillian could not disagree. The lunchroom, once a happy place of laughter and food and animated conversation, had turned into a quiet room where even the crinkling sound of cellophane and paper bags had become muted and dull. Everyone dreaded getting The Call, and with good reason. Cerise's parents had grounded her for three solid weeks based on the information they received from the Dumpling Man, which was that Cerise had thrown seven uneaten apples directly into the trash.

Now the Dumpling Man was approaching their own table.

Snap.

That was the first half of a baby carrot. Quickly, Bonwit and Cerise and Julia Gillian turned their attention to their lunches. Cerise had chosen the cold lunch option today, which consisted of a cheese sandwich, an orange, and a plastic-sealed oatmeal cookie.

Crunch.

That was the other half of the baby carrot.

Bonwit upended his plastic *Star Tribune* bag, spilling its contents onto the table: a granola bar, a container of pineapple yogurt, and an orange. Julia Gillian looked on in consternation. Bonwit's lunches used to be creative. Every day he used to bring a different kind of sandwich on a different kind of bread, and occasionally, he used to bring a small Thermos filled with soup or pasta. Bonwit's lunches had long been the envy of the lunchroom.

"Why are you staring?" said Bonwit.

There was a somewhat defiant tone in his voice, which was also unlike Bonwit.

"Is that really your lunch?" said Julia Gillian.

"Of course it's my lunch."

"It doesn't look like the kind you usually bring."

"Well," said Bonwit, "it is today."

His tone was short, and Julia Gillian decided not to pursue the matter. She opened her own lunch in its brown paper bag.

"What's your note say today?" said Bonwit, who was gloomily spooning up his pineapple yogurt with a plastic spoon.

Bonwit's yogurt had been sitting in his locker all morning, which meant that it must be lukewarm. Julia

Gillian did not enjoy lukewarm yogurt, and it did not look as if Bonwit was enjoying his, either.

"No note," said Julia Gillian. "Remember? I make my own lunches now, too."

Bonwit nodded in a dispirited way. Cerise took a listless bite of her cheese sandwich, which did not look as if it had either mustard or mayonnaise on it. Oh, for the days of Mrs. K, when Oreos abounded and mustard and mayonnaise flowed aplenty.

"It's a reign of terror," Bonwit said suddenly. He was bent over his lukewarm pineapple yogurt, and his voice was quiet. "That's what this is."

This was such an unusual thing for Bonwit to say that both Cerise and Julia Gillian turned to him in surprise.

"And it's got to change," said Bonwit. "I don't know how, but it's got to change."

This, too, was something new. Julia Gillian and Cerise looked at each other over Bonwit's bent head.

"I mean, we're only in fifth grade," said Bonwit. "We're going to be in middle school next year, which means that we have another three years here at Lake Harriet. What if Mrs. K's ankle never gets any better? What if we're stuck with the Dumpling Man forever?"

This was an awful thought. Next year they would be sixth-graders. All their classes would be with different teachers each hour, up on the second floor of the building, which was the sole and hallowed territory of the sixth- and seventh-graders. This was frightening enough to contemplate, but it would be far worse in the continued presence of the Dumpling Man. Darkness permeated the school. Where was the joy?

"I have an idea," said Julia Gillian. It had come to her just then, like a flash of light. "Let's draw up a petition."

"A petition?" said Bonwit.

"Yes. We'll call it the Lake Harriet Anti-Wintz Petition."

Everyone looked at one another. Murmurs rose from the tables within earshot. The students were familiar with petitions, because they had to sign them in support of Student Council candidates. Petitions were formal documents. Julia Gillian pictured herself presenting the Lake Harriet Anti-Wintz Petition to the Supreme Court in Washington, DC. This was a pleasant image, and it spurred Julia Gillian on.

CHAPTER TEN
The Snortlike Laugh

Julia Gillian and Bonwit still met by the teachers' parking lot every day after school, and they still walked side by side all the way to 36th and Dupont, and they still looked both ways at the Intersection of Fear. But the easy conversation was gone. Julia Gillian had still not been invited over to Bonwit's, and Bonwit often looked grim.

"How's your mother's cold?" Julia Gillian said now.

"The same."

They had passed the Intersection of Fear and were approaching 36th Street. A large stick obscured part of the curb cut. Julia Gillian reached down to toss it aside, using more force than necessary.

145

"Why don't you just tell me the truth, Bonwit?" said Julia Gillian. "Why don't you just tell me that you don't want to be part of The One and Onlys anymore?"

Oh dear. Julia Gillian had not planned to say this, but she couldn't take her words back now. She could feel Bonwit staring at her, but she was afraid to look at him.

"I do," said Bonwit. "That's the problem. I do want to be part of The One and Onlys."

Here they were at 36th and Dupont, where Bonwit turned right and she turned left. Was he not going to say a word? Julia

Gillian was still afraid to look at Bonwit,
but she looked at him anyway.

He was pale, and he looked tired. Suddenly
Julia Gillian thought of him at lunch, spooning
up his lukewarm pineapple yogurt.

"Then why don't you ever want me to come
to your house?"

"I do want you to come to my
house."

"Then why do you keep saying
your mother has a cold?"

Julia Gillian was not a person
given much to anger, but her voice
sounded harsh.

"Because she's sick. She doesn't feel good."

"Colds don't last a month, Bonwit."

"Some do," he said quickly. "Some colds last a long time."

Julia Gillian shook her head. She just wanted the truth, and Bonwit was keeping it from her. Now it occurred to her that she was also keeping the truth from him. What had happened to them?

The next day at trumpet lessons, Bonwit took his customary seat next to Julia Gillian. By habit, she turned to him so that they could discuss the events of the lunchroom — today, the lunch man had confiscated a granola bar from a third-grader — but then she remembered things were difficult between them now. Bonwit turned to her, though, with an anxious look on his face.

"Can you play 'Song of My Soul' yet?" he whispered.

Julia Gillian didn't know what to say. No, she could not play "Song of My Soul" yet. She couldn't even play a single note, let alone an entire song.

"Because I can't," said Bonwit.

In ordinary times, Julia Gillian would focus immediately on her best friend's unhappiness and try to make him feel better. These were not ordinary times, though, and she had weightier things on her mind.

"The beginning's okay, and the middle isn't too bad," said Bonwit. "But I can't get the ending right. It sounds terrible. Mr. Mixler wasn't kidding when he said it was tricky."

"I'm sure you'll be fine."

Bonwit looked at her in surprise. Julia Gillian could not blame him, as even to her own ears she didn't sound like herself. "I'm sure you'll be fine" was the sort of thing that an adult would say automatically to a child, and Julia Gillian was not an adult.

"Can you play it once through for me?" Bonwit asked. "Just so I can hear how it's supposed to sound?"

"I can't. I accidentally left my trumpet at home."

This, of course, was another lie. There had been

nothing accidental about Julia Gillian's forgetting her trumpet at home. *If only I had one more week to try,* she had thought that morning, and then the idea had come to her.

"Use mine, then," said Bonwit. "Just play it once."

Julia Gillian laughed. She couldn't help herself. Bonwit had just asked her to play "Song of My Soul" so that he could hear how it was supposed to sound. Truly, he was asking the wrong person. Bonwit drew back and looked at her with an odd expression on his face.

"Are you laughing at me?" he said.

Julia Gillian laughed again. She couldn't help it. There was nothing funny about the situation, and there was nothing funny about her laugh, either. Mr. Mixler

came bounding into the music room. At first he looked at her, smiling, as if he wanted in on the joke, but then his smile faded and he looked puzzled.

"Ms. Gillian? Where is your trumpet?"

She wanted to answer, but she couldn't stop laughing. This didn't even sound like a laugh. It was a harsh snort unlike any laugh Julia Gillian could remember herself making. This was very embarrassing.

"My goodness," said Mr. Mixler. "Someone has found the joy."

He was smiling, but he also looked a little nervous. Julia Gillian's laughter was not the laughter of someone who had found the joy. The other trumpet students looked askance at her. Finally she managed to stop laughing by staring down at her trumpetless lap, but she could still feel the strange snort inside her for the rest of the lesson, ready to burst forth.

"What happened to you today at trumpet lessons?" said Bonwit.

They were back in Ms. Schultz's room, waiting for the final bell to ring. Outside, the sky was the color it turned only in fall, and if it were a normal time, Julia Gillian would admire its deep blueness. But this was a time of downcastness, and she kept her head down, focusing on the Vince Rules the Universe inscription gouged under her desktop.

"I couldn't stop laughing," said Julia Gillian.

That, at least, was the truth.

"But why were you laughing?"

"I don't know."

This was also the truth, but it was not very reassuring. Bonwit zipped up his backpack, into which he had packed all his schoolbooks. It wasn't necessary to carry them all home every day — the ones you didn't need could be stored in your locker — but it had long been Bonwit's custom to do so. He loved books, even textbooks, and he liked having them nearby at all times.

"Were you laughing at me?"

There was the question again. Julia Gillian had been laughing so hard in the music room that she had not been able to answer Bonwit, but she was not laughing now.

"No."

"Are you sure?"

Bonwit's voice was quiet again, the way it had been in the music room.

"Yes."

Julia Gillian was keeping her answers short, and thus far she hadn't lied once. Maybe that was the key. Maybe she could keep her answers short and concise for the rest of her life, and then she wouldn't be so much of a liar.

"You *were* laughing at me, weren't you?" said Bonwit. "You were laughing at me because I can't get the ending of 'Song of My Soul' right."

"No."

"Yes."

"No."

"Yes."

This was getting them nowhere, and Julia Gillian decided not to say another word. Bonwit must have decided the same thing, because he, too, fell silent. They were silent until the bell rang, and they were silent all the way down Upton, and they were silent as they looked both ways at the Intersection of Fear, and they were silent the whole way home.

CHAPTER ELEVEN
Dog Park Ho!

"Noodlie!"

Julia Gillian looked up to see Enzo leaning out her window, watching her approach.

"Noodlie!"

"Hi, Enzo."

Julia Gillian's voice sounded preoccupied, even to her own ears, but she was truly not in the mood for conversation, not even with Enzo, whom she loved. It had been a long day, and she had a great deal on her mind.

"Dog park ho!" said Enzo, and she smiled.

Ordinarily, Julia Gillian would be thrilled to hear these words. This meant that instead of their usual ten-square-block constitutional, she and Bigfoot would be allowed to walk to the dog park in the company of Enzo. Julia Gillian loved the dog park, and so did Bigfoot. All manner of dogs could be found in the dog park, and Julia Gillian liked to sit on one of the benches and observe them. Bigfoot liked to walk the perimeter of the dog park, inspecting the benches and trees and sniffing at bedraggled tennis balls and left-behind Frisbees.

"I called your parents," said Enzo. "They said it would be fine."

"Okay," said Julia Gillian.

She trudged up the stairs to her apartment, where Bigfoot was not at the door to greet her. This in itself was not a good sign, as Bigfoot was almost always standing at the door when she opened it, his tail wagging, his eyes bright with happiness to see her. Was even Bigfoot losing faith in her? She plodded down the hall to her bedroom, where Bigfoot, bat under his paw, was asleep on his long magenta pillow. He opened one eye and heaved himself to his feet.

"Come on, Bigfoot. Dog park ho."

There was puzzlement in Bigfoot's eyes, and Julia Gillian could not blame him. After all, it was a rare treat to be able to go to the dog park. Yet here was Julia Gillian, speaking of the dog park in the same dull voice she spoke of trumpet practice. For Bigfoot's sake, Julia Gillian decided to try again.

"Dog park ho!" she said in what she hoped was a sprightly voice.

But Bigfoot still gazed up at her in puzzlement. He knew when Julia Gillian was not telling the truth in word or deed, and this was one of those times.

I give up, thought Julia Gillian, and she clipped Bigfoot's leash to his collar and trudged back down the stairs to where Enzo was waiting on the sidewalk.

"Are you ready, Noodlie?"

"Yes."

Julia Gillian was so distracted by her problems that she barely noticed her usual dog park walk landmarks. She and Enzo and Bigfoot passed the house of the lovely hillside garden without comment, even though both owners were working in the chrysanthemum patch surrounded by their three Bernese mountain dogs.

Julia Gillian usually liked observing Bernese mountain dogs, which were big — although not nearly as big as Bigfoot — and interesting-looking, with their clownish brown, black, and white faces.

They passed the tiny Grace Nursery School garden on the Greenway, with its miniature bridge and miniature bench. Sometimes, in late spring, Enzo and Bigfoot and Julia Gillian passed by just at the right time, so that they were able to observe the Grace Nursery School students digging in the dirt, zipping over the miniature bridge, and planting the flowers that they had been growing inside since February. Julia Gillian had once been a student at Grace herself, although that had been long ago, in pregarden days. She had loved Grace Nursery School, particularly the sand table and the double tricycle, which she and her friends used to ride around and around in circles.

"I used to love Grace Nursery School," she said.

"Did you?" said Enzo. "Goodness knows I love Metropolitan State. I love my Shakespeare class, I love my Intermedia Arts class, and I love my Algebra for Liberal Arts Majors class."

Thinking about her classes at Metropolitan State University made Enzo so happy that she did a little twirl, right there on the Greenway. It made Julia Gillian sad to witness how much Enzo loved school. She, too, had once loved school, but no longer. Luckily, they were at the dog park now, and Julia Gillian could focus on Bigfoot, whose tail was wagging faster than usual in anticipation. Julia Gillian unclipped his leash and he looked up at her, bat dangling from his jaws.

"Do you want me to keep your bat safe for you, Bigfoot?" she said.

She put out her hand, and Bigfoot let the bat drop into her palm. She wasn't fond of Bigfoot's bat, but she would do anything to make her dog happy, and if that meant protecting his drooly, battered bat, then so be it.

The dog park was busy today. The tiered water-bowl stand was crowded with small and large dogs lapping away. Tennis balls flew through the air, and a line of dogs streaked about the perimeter of the park. Bigfoot gazed around happily, his tail thumping on the ground.

"Well, I never," said Enzo, who was fond of old-time sayings. "I do believe that is my old classmate."

She pointed across the park at a man jumping up and down near the large mulberry tree. This was odd behavior for a nondog, and Julia Gillian watched with interest until she realized that the man was trying to reach a Frisbee wedged between two branches just out of his reach. A dog nearby waited patiently, his head moving up and down with the motions of the jumping.

"Wintz!" called Enzo. "Wintz?"

She waved her arm. Across the park, the jumping man was squinting and tilting his head, trying to figure out the identity of this waving woman.

"Enzo!" he called.

His voice was familiar. Now Enzo and the man were making their way toward each other, picking their way through the muddy patches and wood chips. Now Julia Gillian was watching as Enzo shook hands with the man with the familiar voice. Julia Gillian felt an icy prickle in her stomach.

Could it be?

It could.

The man with the familiar voice was the Dumpling Man.

Julia Gillian instinctively stood up straight —
posture! — and looked around for a place to hide. The
thought of the Dumpling Man recognizing her was more
than she could bear. The dog park was wide open,
though, with only the mulberry tree and a spindly oak
for cover.

"Noodlie!"

Enzo waved and smiled, beckoning Julia Gillian over
to where she and the Dumpling Man stood by the far
bench. The Dumpling Man turned in the direction of
Julia Gillian and squinted. Immediately, Julia Gillian
looked down at the ground, which was covered in
wood chips. It had rained recently, and the wood chips
were damp.

"Noodlie!"

Enzo's voice was louder. Julia Gillian kept her eyes focused on a small, brown hard-backed bug that was attempting to make its way over a knobby chip. She watched as it climbed and fell back, climbed and fell back. Poor little thing. Even if the bug did manage to summit the chip, there were hundreds — no, thousands, maybe even millions — of other chips in the dog park. This bug could have no idea of the enormity of the obstacles it faced. This bug, poor thing, was living a life parallel to Julia Gillian's life. She bent down, the better to hide herself from the gaze of the Dumpling Man.

"Poodle!"

Oh no. The dreaded Poodle nickname was being used, and Enzo's voice was louder still, not to mention

annoyed. The longer she stayed at the dog park, the sooner the Dumpling Man would recognize her.

There was only one thing to do.

"Come on, Bigfoot," said Julia Gillian, and she marched quickly to the gate. Bigfoot followed her, but his tail was no longer wagging. Julia Gillian clipped the leash to his collar and opened the gate. A Great Dane was approaching the exterior gate, but Julia Gillian did not stop.

"Home," she said to Bigfoot, and off they went without looking back. Quick to the gate, quick with the leash, quick onto the Greenway.

"Poodle!"

"Come on, Bigfoot!"

"Poodle!"

Enzo was fast. Extremely fast.

"What in the world do you think you're doing, Poodle?"

Julia Gillian thought fast. There was only one thing that could excuse her behavior, and that was sickness. She bent over and held her stomach. Immediately, Enzo's arm was around her.

"Julia Gillian? Are you sick?"

Miserably, Julia Gillian nodded. Another lie. Not only that, but a lie to Enzo, her treasured friend. Julia Gillian *did* feel sick, but not to her stomach. If only she could tell Enzo everything, from the beginning.

"Where does it hurt?" said Enzo.

Julia Gillian just shook her head. It hurt everywhere, she thought. Now she could feel Enzo looking at her in her Enzo way. She didn't say anything, though. Julia Gillian's father would say that Enzo's steel-trap-like mind was figuring everything out, *click click click.* They walked down the Greenway in silence, with Bigfoot padding along beside them. Enzo knew Julia Gillian very well, and this silence could mean only one thing: Enzo was on to her.

It was a long walk home.

CHAPTER TWELVE

Help Me, Vince

The lunchroom was quiet. Julia Gillian's mother had made her ants on a log, which she usually enjoyed because of the satisfying *crunch* of the celery. These days, however, crunches served as a reminder of the Dumpling Man and his baby carrots. Julia Gillian selected a log and lined up the ants on it as evenly as possible. *That one a little to the left*, she thought, nudging them into place, *and that one a little to the right.*

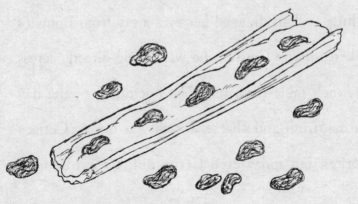

Lathrop was spooning up vanilla pudding from the container that had come with his hot lunch. Ever since his braces, pudding, which was soft and required no chewing, had become one of Lathrop's foods. He ate mechanically, one spoonful after another, without even looking up. Meanwhile, Bonwit had pulled an apple out of his lunch and was tossing it gently from hand to hand as if he were a one-apple juggler. First one hand, then the other. Back and forth, and back and forth, and back and forth.

Julia Gillian dragged her eyes away from Bonwit's apple tossing to Cerise, who was sitting directly across the lunch table from her. The hot lunch of the day was macaroni and cheese, which was one of Cerise's favorites, but today even Cerise didn't seem hungry.

She was concentrating on threading one macaroni onto each of her plastic fork tines. This was difficult — the macaroni kept splitting — but eventually Cerise triumphed.

"Look," she said, waving her macaroni-laden fork in the air.

"There will be no playing with food in the Lake Harriet lunchroom," said the Dumpling Man.

He stood directly behind Cerise, his arms folded across his Keep on Truckin' T-shirt, which he wore at least once a week. Cerise had been so focused on her task that despite the quiet of the lunchroom, she had missed the sound of his footsteps. Now she lowered her macaroni fork. Bonwit stopped tossing his apple and looked down at his lunch bag, which today was a Lund's plastic bag, slightly ripped, but not enough that Bonwit's lunch spilled out. Lathrop kept spooning up his vanilla pudding.

The Dumpling Man dipped his hand into his bag of baby carrots and extracted one. *Snap.* Julia Gillian broke off a small piece of her granola bar and pushed it onto one of her ants on a log, exactly halfway between two raisins. *Good job, little granola ball*, she beamed telepathically. She kept her finger on the little granola ball and looked up at the lunch man, who had paused with the remaining half of his baby carrot halfway to his mouth.

"Excuse me," said the lunch man. "Maybe you didn't hear me. There will be no playing with food in this lunchroom."

"Why not?" said Julia Gillian.

"Why not what?"

"Why will there be no playing with food in the Lake Harriet lunchroom?"

The quiet lunchroom became quieter.

"Because no playing with food is a school rule," said the lunch man.

"Well, then, I'd like to see the bylaws."

"Excuse me?"

The lunch man looked surprised. Julia Gillian herself was surprised. She had no idea what bylaws were. She had no idea where she had plucked the word *bylaws* from, but it sounded official and legal. The Dumpling Man unfolded and refolded his arms. *Courage*, thought Julia Gillian, and she pictured her fierce raccoon mask, which was even now hanging in her locker.

The Dumpling Man's ever-present bag of carrots was half-empty. It was rumored that eating too many baby carrots could turn you orange. Julia Gillian looked at her own arms, then back at the Dumpling Man's. His arms did seem slightly yellow.

"Excuse me?" he said again.

"The bylaws," repeated Julia Gillian. "It's my right to examine the bylaws of my own school."

Bonwit and Cerise and Lathrop looked at Julia Gillian, then at each other, then back at her. Julia Gillian was full of surprises these days.

"What are bylaws?" Bonwit said to Julia Gillian.

They were back in Ms. Schultz's classroom, waiting for the bell to ring for next hour. Which happened to be Trumpet. Which Julia Gillian was not thinking about just now.

"I don't really know," she said. "Something to do with rules. It sounded good though, didn't it? We should add it to the Lake Harriet Anti-Wintz Petition."

The other students nodded. Until now, if she had to guess which student would be most likely to stand up to the Dumpling Man, Cerise would have been the natural choice. But it had not been Cerise. It had been Julia Gillian.

"I had to do it," Julia Gillian said. "I couldn't take it anymore."

"It's a reign of terror," agreed Bonwit.

Julia Gillian looked down at the Vince Rules the Universe inscription under her desktop. Was it possible that Vince was still alive somewhere, all these years after he had gouged his name into the wood of her desk? Perhaps he was an old man now, walking the streets of Minneapolis with a cane, although not a dog-head cane. Julia Gillian found this thought comforting. *Help me, Vince*, she beamed to the old man Vince, wandering the streets of Minneapolis.

Ms. Schultz was busy at the board, erasing the day's work. It was time for the class to gather their books and organize their backpacks, to get ready for the final bell.

"Where's our petition?" said Julia Gillian.

"In my locker," said Bonwit.

"Go get it."

"Now?"

"The time has come," said Julia Gillian.

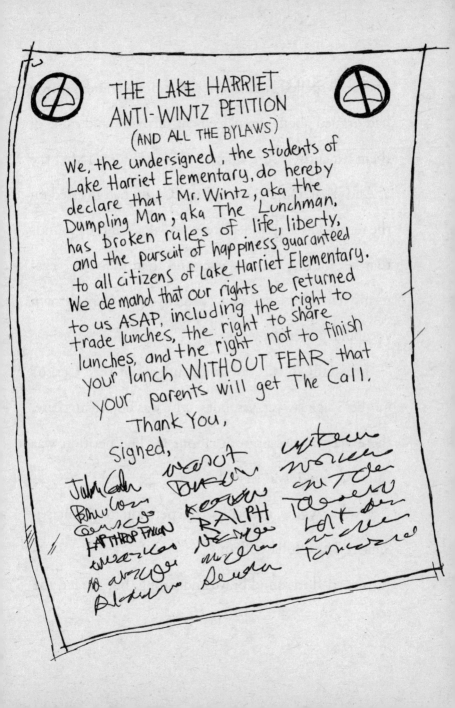

THE LAKE HARRIET
ANTI-WINTZ PETITION
(AND ALL THE BYLAWS)

We, the undersigned, the students of
Lake Harriet Elementary, do hereby
declare that Mr. Wintz, aka the
Dumpling Man, aka The Lunchman,
has broken rules of life, liberty,
and the pursuit of happiness guaranteed
to all citizens of Lake Harriet Elementary.
We demand that our rights be returned
to us ASAP, including the right to
trade lunches, the right to share
lunches, and the right not to finish
your lunch WITHOUT FEAR that
your parents will get The Call.

Thank You,

Signed,

Had they spelled *guaranteed* right? Bonwit and Lathrop had argued about the placement of the *u*, and none of them felt entirely sure whether it went before or after the *a*. And what about the wording? Cerise had insisted on the terms "do hereby declare" and "aka" on the grounds that her mother was a lawyer and that, therefore, legal terms had trickled down correctly into Cerise's own vocabulary over the years.

Julia Gillian was not at all sure about this. Cerise's mother was a lawyer, yes, but Cerise was not. In any case, there was no use arguing about it. The petition was finished, and it was signed.

"Who wants to bring the petition to Principal Smartt?" said Julia Gillian.

She tried to sound brave and strong, but in fact, the

idea of bringing the petition to the principal's office was intimidating. The students looked frightened, and she could not blame them.

"All you have to do is slip it under the door," she added encouragingly.

Still, no one raised a hand. And that was how it happened that, when the bell rang for trumpet lessons, Julia Gillian found herself taking a circuitous route to Mr. Mixler's class, one that included a brief detour by Principal Smartt's office. She was surprised at how easy it was to send the petition sailing under the door. Just a little flick of her hand was all it took.

CHAPTER THIRTEEN

With Her Trumpet
in Her Lap

"My trumpeters!" Mr. Mixler said now. The Mixler baton flew back and forth in the air to a happy dance of its own invention. "How did practice go this past week?"

"Great!"

"Great!"

"Great!"

This was the way it was in Julia Gillian's life now. Everything was great for everyone except her.

"Great!" said Mr. Mixler. "Are we ready for 'Song of My Soul'!"

He was especially buoyant today. Each of his

sentences, including his questions, seemed to end in an exclamation mark. "Song of My Soul" was not an exclamation mark sort of song, at least in Julia Gillian's opinion, but Mr. Mixler's enthusiasm was contagious, and the students responded in kind.

"Yes!"

"Yes!"

"Why not!"

Julia Gillian said nothing. There was no escape now. She had been spared thus far by a series of unusual events — the fire drill, the end-of-class bell, pretending to be ill, and her own snorting laughter — but there was no reasonable hope that anything else would come along to save her.

What would happen to her, once she was discovered to be a trumpet fraud? She imagined Mr. Mixler's face, how it would fall in disappointment and disbelief: Here was a girl that he had believed in as both a trumpet student and a human being, and all this time she had been lying. Perhaps he would confiscate her trumpet immediately. It was a school trumpet, after all.

The Mixler baton halted its happy little dance and came to rest in the air.

"Trumpets up!"

Trumpets up.

"A one and a two and a three!"

The five trumpet students who could actually make sounds on their trumpets played "Song of My Soul." Julia Gillian, as had become her habit, blew quietly into her trumpet without a sound, her fingers moving in unison with Bonwit's next to her. Near the end, Bonwit gave her a strange look. Did he know the truth?

"Very good!" said Mr. Mixler when each trumpet had played the last, lingering note.

"No," said Bonwit, next to Julia Gillian.

He lay his trumpet in his lap and looked up at Mr. Mixler.

"Excuse me, Mr. Keller?" said Mr. Mixler.

"I'm sorry, Mr. Mixler," said Bonwit again.

His foot tapped out a light rhythm on the tiled floor of the music room. Julia Gillian had known Bonwit since kindergarten, and she knew that this was a sign he was nervous. He was nervous because he knew. He knew that she, Julia Gillian, his best friend, had been lying ever since the beginning of trumpet lessons. Bonwit was about to expose her to Mr. Mixler and the other students.

"Is something amiss, Mr. Keller?" said Mr. Mixler.

He looked expectantly at Bonwit and waited. All the trumpet students were looking at Bonwit with interest. What could the problem be? She felt dizzy. She could not believe that Bonwit was about to reveal the truth about her in front of Mr. Mixler and the other students. This was not the way a best friend should behave.

Courage, thought Julia Gillian, picturing her dear raccoon mask, hanging on the back hook in her locker.

She raised her hand. Now Mr. Mixler, along with everyone else, shifted his gaze in order to look at Julia Gillian. Bonwit turned and stared at her, too. What was she doing?

"Yes, Ms. Gillian?"

"It's me. I can't play 'Song of My Soul.'"

Mr. Mixler lowered his baton.

"You mean you're having difficulty with the tricky ending?"

"Not just the tricky ending. I'm having difficulty with everything."

Now Mr. Mixler tilted his head in confusion, and so did the other trumpet students. Julia Gillian could feel Bonwit staring at her. She had finally admitted the truth.

"I can't play my trumpet at all," said Julia Gillian. "I can't even make a single sound."

CHAPTER FOURTEEN
The Intersection of Fear

Julia Gillian did not return to Ms. Schultz's class after lessons. Instead, she hid in the restroom next to the lunchroom. She pictured the look on Bonwit's face when she admitted she couldn't make a sound. She pictured the surprise on Mr. Mixler's face, and the way he had lowered the Mixler baton. Her secret was out now, and she felt too embarrassed to have her friends see her, a baby who couldn't even make a single sound on her trumpet.

By skipping class, she realized that she was breaking another school rule, but these were desperate times. She sat in the far stall next to the window, listening to the sounds of lockers slamming, feet thudding on the stairs, and the laughter of children heading home for the weekend.

There was a time when Julia Gillian would have been one of those children. She and Bonwit would have met after school at their appointed meeting place by the teachers' parking lot. They would have walked home together and made their plans for the weekend: free-throw practice at Julia Gillian's house, an art project, dinner and a strawberry bubble tea at the Quang Vietnamese Restaurant. That had all changed now, and in only a few weeks.

"Ms. Gillian," Mr. Mixler had said when the ending

bell rang. "Would it be possible for you to meet me before school on Monday morning?"

The other trumpet students, including Bonwit, had studiously avoided looking at her, but she knew that everyone had heard what Mr. Mixler said. She had nodded. What else could she do? Her failure was now known to all. She had sat in silence with her trumpet in her lap, disgraced, for the rest of the lesson.

Now Julia Gillian's trumpet was on her lap again, carefully packed in its black vinyl case. Mr. Mixler would probably be requesting its return when they met before school on Monday. She felt sorry for her trumpet, and she felt sorry for herself.

Julia Gillian sat in the stall until all the outside

sounds had faded. On the extreme off-chance that Bonwit was still in the vicinity, she decided to slip out the side door by the playground. She pictured Bonwit, making his way toward home on Sheridan Avenue. Perhaps he was scuffling through the leaves, his head down. Now he knew that she had been keeping this enormous secret for an entire month. What must he be thinking?

Julia Gillian took a deep breath, stood up, and left the restroom. She headed down the hall to the stairs and made her way up to the first-floor playground door. The halls were deserted. There was something sad about a school with no children in it.

"Hello."

Julia Gillian did not even have to turn around to know who that voice belonged to. But she did turn around, and there sat the Dumpling Man, cross-legged, next to the drinking fountain. His bag of carrots was in his lap, and so was a piece of paper that Julia Gillian immediately recognized as the Lake Harriet Anti-Wintz Petition.

From this vantage point, the Dumpling Man did not look as fierce as he usually did. He was wearing his Dumpling Man T-shirt today, and the crudely drawn dumpling was half-hidden in a fold. He withdrew a baby carrot and bit off half. The crunching of the baby carrot was quite loud in the silent hall. How many carrots could one person eat?

"You're the bylaws girl," said the Dumpling Man.

"Indeed I am," said Julia Gillian automatically.

The Dumpling Man studied the remaining half of his baby carrot.

"Tell me something," he said. "Do the kids despise me?"

He poked at the Anti-Wintz Petition. Julia Gillian was standing straight up, looking down on the Dumpling Man, who now looked quite small and much younger than she would have thought.

"Do they? You can tell me the truth."

"Well," said Julia Gillian carefully. "They *are* a little afraid of you."

The Dumpling Man blinked.

"I guess they must be, judging from this," he said, waving the petition in the air.

Julia Gillian nodded. The Dumpling Man popped the other half of his baby carrot into his mouth and stared up at her.

"I wasn't a good student when I was a kid," he said now. "I didn't abide by the rules. I didn't listen to authority. I spent a lot of time in the principal's office."

He pulled another baby carrot out of his bag and held it in the air between thumb and forefinger, studying it as if it were an unfamiliar sight.

"When I got this job, I wanted to do it right," he said. "I wanted to follow the rules. I wanted to make up for the past."

He waved the petition in the air.

"But here I am," he said. "Called into the principal's office again."

He stared at the petition and bit into his baby carrot.

"I tried so hard," he said again. "But I still failed."

Julia Gillian pictured his military march up and down the rows of lunchroom tables, and the silence and good posture left in his wake. She pictured the very first day of his reign of terror, and how she had crammed Bonwit's Oreo into her mouth.

And now here sat the Dumpling Man, crunching

sadly on his baby carrots. She did not know what to say. They were both trying to do a good job, and they were both failing. Who would have thought that there would be any similarities between Julia Gillian and the Dumpling Man? But there it was. Things were more complicated than she had imagined.

Her conversation with the Dumpling Man had made Julia Gillian forget that she had stayed after school in order to avoid Bonwit. So when she pushed open the side door to the playground, it was a shock to find him waiting for her there.

"I thought you might come out this door," he said.

"How did you know I was still here?"

"I just knew."

Bonwit was carrying his trumpet in front of him, clasped in both arms as if it were a baby. His red backpack, crammed to capacity, hung low on his back.

For a while they walked in silence, occasionally scuffling their feet to kick up a particularly good pile of leaves. The squirrels were especially busy today, noted Julia Gillian, dashing back and forth across the streets with their cheeks stuffed full of nuts. It was that time of year, when all squirrels needed to be vigilant about storing up nuts for the oncoming winter. She did worry about them, the way they never looked in either direction when crossing the street. What good would all the nuts in the world do a squirrel if he were pancaked in the middle of the road? Ordinarily, Julia Gillian would make this observation to Bonwit as they walked home together — they shared a concern for the heedless squirrels — but she said nothing.

They were closing in on the Intersection of Fear before either of them spoke.

"That was brave of you today," said Bonwit.

No it wasn't, thought Julia Gillian.

"How did you have the guts?"

I don't have the guts, thought Julia Gillian.

"In front of everyone and everything," said Bonwit. "Just to come right out and tell him you couldn't play a single note."

"Well, I knew that you were about to tell everyone," said Julia Gillian. "So I told them first."

Bonwit stared at her.

"I didn't even know you couldn't make a sound," he said. "I was going to tell Mr. Mixler that I don't know how to play the ending of 'Song of My Soul.'"

Usually, Bonwit and Julia Gillian were the same height. But today, with his extra-heavy backpack in back and his trumpet clutched before him, Bonwit seemed to have shrunk a few inches.

"And you were brave in the lunchroom, too," said Bonwit. "You just stood right up to the Dumpling Man."

He shook his head.

"You've changed," he said.

"I have not," said Julia Gillian. "But *you* have."

Now they were at the Intersection of Fear. Julia Gillian jumped back as a car screeched around the curve on a red light, its driver in a hurry and unwilling to wait. Other cars began turning on their green arrows. The Intersection of Fear was a complicated one, full of green arrows, yellow arrows, and red lights. Julia Gillian reached out and pressed the Walk button again.

"You're brave," Bonwit said again.

Here was Bonwit, telling her that she had changed, and that she was brave, when in fact Julia Gillian was not at all brave. This had to stop. The light turned green and the little white walking man appeared. Julia Gillian turned to look for cars crossing against the light, which would not be unheard of here at the Intersection of Fear.

"I'm not brave," said Bonwit.

His voice sounded strange, and Julia Gillian saw that he was crying. The light was still green, and the little white walking man still shone, and they crossed the street. There was the giant wood-chip pile by the lake, free to any Minneapolis resident for the taking. Sometimes, on bitter winter days, Bonwit and Julia Gillian liked to climb to the top of the wood-chip pile and let the warmth rise through their boots.

Now, without looking at each other, and even though this was not a bitter winter day, they climbed to the top of the wood-chip pile. Julia Gillian did not know what to do. The fact that her best friend was crying made her want to cry, too. And then she *was* crying.

Julia Gillian was crying because she couldn't play the trumpet. Because she missed her tiny folded lunch notes. Because she missed being at Bonwit's house, eating cookies and doing art projects together. Because for some reason Bonwit didn't want to be her best friend anymore. Now Bonwit reached up and wiped his face. Julia Gillian didn't know why he was crying, but it hurt to see him sad.

Bonwit shook his head.

"I wish I was still in fourth grade," he said.

"Me too," said Julia Gillian.

CHAPTER FIFTEEN

The End of Her Rope

"Poodle."

Oh no. How much worse could one day get? Standing at the double front doors to her apartment building, Julia Gillian was afraid to raise her eyes. The way Enzo had said *Poodle* — in that stern tone of voice — did not bode well.

I am invisible, thought Julia Gillian. *Invisible am I.*

"Poodle."

Once again, the enchantment of invisibility had not worked, not that it ever had. Julia Gillian raised her eyes to the third floor, where Enzo was leaning out of her window.

She was not waving, nor was she smiling.

"We'll see you upstairs."

This was a command, not a question. Julia Gillian trudged up to her apartment. Bigfoot was waiting for her just inside the door, his tail sweeping slowly from side to side, his head tilted.

"Come on, Bigfoot," said Julia Gillian.

Thank goodness she had Bigfoot. He was always there to give her extra strength. Look at him, her stalwart companion, plodding down the hall after her and down the stairs, his head down, as if he, too, were not looking forward to whatever it was that Enzo had to say.

But it was not just Enzo waiting at her apartment with the door open. Julia Gillian's parents were also there, standing just inside the door. It must be serious if her parents had come home early.

"Hi, honey," said her father.

"Hi, sweetie," said her mother.

They looked concerned and determined. It was obvious that the three of them had been talking, and this could mean nothing good. Enzo was wearing her platform boots, which made her quite a bit taller than Julia Gillian. She inclined her head toward the indoor reading hammock. Julia Gillian took a seat in it as best she could — it was difficult to sit up straight in a hammock, after all — and Enzo sat in her brown velvet chair. Julia Gillian's parents sat on the couch.

Bigfoot stood between them, his head swiveling back and forth and his tail wagging, until Julia Gillian pointed to the floor and he sat down.

"Enzo and your mother and I have been talking, honey," said her father, "and all three of us are worried about you."

Just as Julia Gillian had expected. Her parents had been brought into the mix, and that meant that the three most important adults in her life were all involved. There would be no getting out of it, whatever *it* was.

Images flickered through Julia Gillian's mind, one after another, jumbling up.

Bonwit crying on top of the city wood-chip pile.

Vince Knows All.

The Dumpling Man, who had turned out to be a friend of Enzo.

The silence of the restroom stall.

The many afternoons sitting on her bed with Bigfoot as witness, trying but failing to make a single sound on her trumpet.

The clink of the dog park gate as she and Bigfoot fled, ignoring Enzo's calls.

"We already know about the dog park," said her mother. "You know you're not allowed to leave there without Enzo."

"And we got a call from school today," said her father. "Apparently you've been skipping class."

"One," said Julia Gillian. "One class."

"What is going on?" said Enzo. "Where is the Julia Gillian that we know and love?"

Good question.

Julia Gillian looked down at Bigfoot, who was looking up at her with a sorrowful expression. She had dragged Bigfoot, the dog of her dreams, into this whole mess. More images flickered through her mind. *Vince Rules the Universe*, gouged into her desk in Ms. Schultz's room. The Dumpling Man and his bag of baby carrots, marching up and down the rows of lunch tables. The feel of the Oreo crammed into her mouth on that fateful day, one month ago, when she had first become a rule breaker and a secret-keeper.

"Bonwit was crying today," she said.

Where had that come from? All three adults frowned in surprise. This was obviously not what they expected Julia Gillian to say. They knew Bonwit, if only slightly, but enough to know that crying was not something typical of Bonwit.

"Why?" said her mother.

"His mother has a cold. She's had it for more than a month."

"Wait a minute," said Enzo. "Bonwit's mother has had a cold for more than a month?"

Julia Gillian shrugged. Nobody has a cold for

more than a month, she thought. Enzo should be able to see that the real problem was that Bonwit was lying.

"And he was crying?" said her father.

"Yes. On the wood-chip pile."

"Have you asked him what's really wrong?" said Enzo.

Julia Gillian looked up at Enzo, who was still sitting perfectly straight in her velvet chair. Maybe her daily pretzelization was good for posture.

"Not exactly."

"Why not?"

"Because I know what's wrong," said Julia Gillian. "He's tired of being my best friend. He keeps lying about his mother's stupid cold because he doesn't want me at his house anymore."

"You don't know if he's lied to you," said her mother, exchanging a look with Julia Gillian's father.

Julia Gillian rolled her eyes. This was an extremely rude thing to do, and she knew it, but she did it anyway.

"Maybe he's lying in order to cover up something that's bothering him," said her mother. "Haven't you ever done that?"

"Nope," said Julia Gillian.

Which was a lie in and of itself, but what difference did it make at this point? Enzo drew herself up even straighter, if that was possible, in her brown velvet chair. Her feet in their platform boots were perfectly still, side by side on the floor.

"What about your trumpet lessons?"

Enzo's voice was calm, and she still sat perfectly straight, and her eyes did not blink. This was Enzo at her strongest. Julia Gillian's parents looked confused.

"My trumpet lessons are great," said Julia Gillian.

"Are they?"

From his position on the floor, Bigfoot looked up at Julia Gillian and tilted his head. Julia Gillian could feel Enzo looking straight at her in her Enzo-like way. She forced herself to look away from Bigfoot and meet her gaze. To her surprise, there was no anger or accusation in Enzo's eyes. Instead, there was sympathy, as if she knew how bad Julia Gillian felt.

"Are your trumpet lessons *really* great?" said Enzo.

Julia Gillian shook her head. Her parents still looked confused. Bigfoot closed his eyes and opened them again.

"I didn't think so, Noodlie."

Noodlie. There it was, the nickname of happiness and love. It felt like a long time since Julia Gillian had felt happiness and love. While she knew that her parents loved her, and Bigfoot loved her, and Enzo and Zap loved her, and that there was much to be happy about in her world, nevertheless, life had been difficult lately.

Julia Gillian slumped down in the hammock. She had come to the end of her rope, and the only way out was through. She took a deep breath.

"Mrs. K broke her ankle," said Julia Gillian.

Her voice was dull.

"I broke a federal health regulation. I ate a confiscated Oreo. I'm a failure."

Now it was all coming out. Enzo crossed her legs, listening. Julia Gillian's parents leaned forward on the couch.

"Tell us everything, honey," said her father.

Where could Julia Gillian possibly begin? More images flashed through her mind. This had been a month of surprises, most of them unpleasant. It had

been a month of dashed expectations. It had been a month of silence and secrets. If only she could step out of herself, just for a while, and be someone else. Vince, for example. Vince, in his knickers and cap and quill pen, Vince who lived so long ago, before there were such things as dumpling men, soundless trumpets, and even Oreos.

CHAPTER SIXTEEN

The Lunches of Bonwit's Past

"I'm a rule breaker," said Julia Gillian. "And I'm a liar."

"About what?" said her mother.

"About the trumpet, for one thing. I can't play it. I can't even make a sound."

"Why didn't you tell us?" said her father.

"Because I wanted to solve my problems by myself," said Julia Gillian. "I didn't want to be a baby and ask for help."

"Asking for help when you need it isn't babyish," said Enzo. "It's brave."

Julia Gillian thought about this. Was it true?

"I wish I lived a long time ago," said Julia Gillian. "Like Vince who used to go to Lake Harriet."

"I used to go to Lake Harriet with a boy named Vince," said Enzo.

Her voice didn't sound stern anymore, now that Julia Gillian was finally talking.

"My Vince lived about a hundred years ago," said Julia Gillian. "He had a quill pen."

"My Vince is still alive," said Enzo. "In fact, he's the guy I saw at the dog park the other day."

Julia Gillian stared at Enzo.

"My Vince had a hard time in school," said Enzo. "He never followed the rules. He was always in trouble. He used to gouge his name into the tables and walls. Even the floor. *Vince Knows All.* It didn't matter how many times they sent him to the principal's office. He was obsessed."

Enzo shook her head.

"His name is Vince Wintz, if you can believe it," she said. "That did not make his life easy."

Now she folded her platform boots underneath her, so that she was sitting cross-legged in the brown velvet chair.

"He was cruelly picked on. I know he was stuck with a terrible name, but still. It's all in the attitude. Right, Noodlie?"

Julia Gillian, sitting in the hammock, had the sensation of being slightly outside her own body, as if she were sitting next to herself and looking with interest at the girl with the stunned expression on her face. The

Vince Who Knew All was the Dumpling Man. Could this possibly be?

"Honey?" said her mother. "Are you all right?"

Julia Gillian's two worlds were colliding. She had the overwhelming desire to talk to Bonwit. She looked at her parents and at Enzo.

"Mom and Dad, may I go see Bonwit?"

"Now?" said her father.

Julia Gillian nodded. Enough was enough. It was time to get back on track with her best friend. Enzo and her mother and father looked at her, and then at each other. It seemed that they could sense that Julia Gillian had made up her mind about something. And Bonwit's house was well within her ten-square-block parameters.

"Be back in an hour," said her mother.

♫

KNOCK. KNOCK. KNOCK.

KnockKnockKnock.

Knock. Knock. Knock.

Julia Gillian was so discombobulated from the knowledge she now possessed — the Dumpling Man was Vince? Her Vince of knickers and cap was the Dumpling Man? — that she used her secret Enzo knock on Bonwit's front door.

No one answered, so Julia Gillian knocked again, this time like a normal person.

Knock. Knock. Knock.

She put her ear to the door and listened for sound from within. Did Bonwit know that it was her at the front door, and was he hiding? Had things gone that far? Next to her, Bigfoot suddenly stood straighter and began wagging his tail. As a true dog person, Julia Gillian knew that this meant someone was approaching the door, and that the approaching someone was a person that Bigfoot knew and liked. The door opened.

"Julia Gillian," said Bonwit.

Bonwit looked away from her and down at the doorsill with a certain look on his face. From her own recent life as a secret-keeper, Julia Gillian knew that he was trying to think of something else to cover up what was no longer working, just as she herself had done. This must stop, and it was up to Julia Gillian to make the first move.

"I haven't been a good friend," she said.

Now Bonwit looked at her.

"I haven't been telling the truth," said Julia Gillian. "I lied about making my own lunches. I lied about the trumpet."

There had only been two real lies, she realized. But each lie had spun off a series of smaller lies. Everywhere she turned she was caught in yet another one. Bonwit tilted his head, and next to her, Bigfoot tilted his own in response.

"You lied about making your own lunches?" said Bonwit.

"Yes, I did. My parents still make them for me. I didn't want you to think I was a baby."

Bonwit looked sad. This was not the reaction Julia Gillian had expected. She had thought that he would make fun of her for being the kind of ten-year-old whose parents still made her lunch.

"I wish my mother still made my lunch," said Bonwit. "I wish she still drew her faces of negativity and positivity."

Really? This did not make sense. Julia Gillian had thought that Bonwit liked making his own lunches. Then she pictured him in the lunchroom, with his plastic *Star Tribune* bag and his lukewarm pineapple yogurt. What had happened to the Bonwit lunches of the past?

"Then why did you start making your own?"

"Because my mother is on bed rest. She has to stay in bed."

"Why? Because of a cold?"

Bonwit looked away. He took a deep breath.

"No. Because I'm going to have twin baby sisters."

Julia Gillian stood perfectly still on the other side of the doorsill. Her brain was in high gear today, working overtime, and suddenly she knew what it must feel like to be Enzo, with a mind like a steel trap. *Click click click.* Things were falling into place. Baby sisters? Bed rest?

Bed rest was why Mr. Mixler had asked Bonwit how his mother was faring. Bed rest was the reason Bonwit's mother no longer made his lunches. This was the reason that Julia Gillian's parents had exchanged that look just now, when Julia Gillian brought up the subject of Bonwit's mother.

The image of baby sisters appeared in Julia Gillian's mind, one dressed in a blue jumpsuit, the other in yellow, sitting side by side in a double stroller. In her mind, Julia Gillian offered each a lollipop, and off they went down the sidewalk, waving their lollipops happily, with her and Bonwit each

pushing one handle

of the double

stroller.

"Why aren't you happy about it?" said Julia Gillian.

"Because," said Bonwit. "I like being an only child. I like things just the way they are."

Now Julia Gillian understood. Bonwit liked his happy cookie-smelling art-project home just the way it was. And come to think of it, so did Julia Gillian. She had a flash of sadness, that it was all going to change once the baby sisters were born.

"May I come in?" said Julia Gillian.

Bonwit opened the door.

Julia Gillian hadn't been inside Bonwit's house since the end of school last spring, before he went to Vermont for the summer. Instinctively she took a deep breath.

Bonwit's mother was not only an artist but an excellent cookie baker, and going to Bonwit's house had always meant good things: Triple-Chip Supremes, for example, served on a special plate that Bonwit's mother had painted with watermelons, mugs of Earl Grey tea — a beverage which made Julia Gillian feel grown up — music playing in the background, and many art supplies to use in their class projects. Bonwit's house was always warm and friendly and peaceful and orderly, and now, standing in the entryway, Julia Gillian realized how much she had missed it.

Her dog stood next to her, his body wiggling happily at once again being inside Bonwit's house. Bigfoot never forgot a place he loved.

Now Bonwit looked Julia Gillian straight in the eye.

"Prepare yourself," said Bonwit.

"For what?"

"Things have changed."

They walked into the house. The usual calm and order and smell of cookies were gone. Papers and books were piled here and there, and the kitchen sink was filled with dishes that needed washing. The art supplies were neatly arrayed on their shelves, and Julia Gillian could tell that they had not been used in quite

some time. The usual happy
mess of art-projects-in-the-
making was missing from the
dining room table. There was
no smell of cookies, nor of Earl
Grey tea.

Bonwit looked sadly at Julia
Gillian and she looked sadly
back at him. They headed
straight upstairs to Bonwit's
room, with Bigfoot close
behind. Bonwit shut the door
behind them.

"Things *have* changed," said
Julia Gillian.

It was all she could think of to say. She sat on Bonwit's bed, and Bigfoot turned around on Bonwit's rug and lay down with his head slumped over his paws. Bonwit sat in the little chair that had been his fourth-birthday present. His mother had made it and then painted it in black and white zebralike stripes. Bonwit had long ago outgrown the chair, but both he and Julia Gillian still liked to sit on it on occasion. Bonwit's mother had been promising to create a new, larger chair for some time, but it seemed clear to Julia Gillian that she would have no time for such a project, given the bed rest and the soon-to-be twin baby girls.

Julia Gillian looked at the silent, drooping Bigfoot,

and the silent, drooping Bonwit, who was plucking at the top of the shoe box that held his interesting-rock collection. She felt terrible. How he must have missed his lunch bag faces of negativity and positivity, just as she had missed reading her tiny folded lunch notes. Two best friends, and yet they had been keeping these big secrets from each other.

"I'm so sorry, Bonwit. I had no idea about your twin baby sisters."

"I'm sorry, too. I had no idea about your trumpet."

"Why didn't we tell each other?"

"I couldn't. I like being a One and Only."

"Well, we've both always liked being One and Onlys," said Julia Gillian.

"Everyone thinks I'm supposed to be so happy about the twins, but I'm not. I feel like a terrible person."

"So do I," said Julia Gillian. "I lied to you about my lunches, and I lied to you about the trumpet."

It felt so good to finally tell the truth. She looked at Bonwit, crammed into his little zebra chair. He looked at her, slumped on the bed. On the floor, Bigfoot twitched a foot and sighed deeply in his sleep. They were all three of them a bunch of sad sacks, as Zap would say.

Suddenly, Julia Gillian had the urge to laugh. She fought this urge valiantly, as this was a serious moment, and to laugh would simply be rude. This felt like a real laugh, though, nothing like the uncontrollable snorting of two weeks ago in Mr. Mixler's class. She looked down and tried to think of something extremely sad, something so sad that her urge to laugh would be driven away entirely.

Just then Bonwit looked up and met her gaze. He was pressing his lips together. They were so firmly pressed that they were turning white, and Julia Gillian observed this with interest. How unusual. Just then, Bonwit burst out with a big honk of laughter, which was so unlike Bonwit that Julia Gillian shrieked in surprise. Bonwit tried to stand up mid-honk, but his zebra chair came with him, which made Julia Gillian laugh so hard that she fell off the bed. This woke Bigfoot up, and he began to bark, which was a very rare occurrence.

Oh my goodness, it felt good to laugh. But now that all their secrets were out, nothing seemed sad anymore. If Mr. Mixler were there, he would dance his baton through the air and say that they had found the joy.

"No more secrets," said Bonwit.

"No more secrets," said Julia Gillian.

"Pinky swear?"

"Pinky swear."

Julia Gillian felt sorry for
grown-ups, who had only their boring
handshakes to depend on. There was nothing better than
a pinky swear, in her opinion, and Bonwit agreed.

CHAPTER SEVENTEEN
Trumpet Up

On Monday morning, Julia Gillian's father dropped her off at school half an hour early, as she had requested. After the laugh attack at Bonwit's house, she had told her parents everything: the whole awful story of trumpet lessons, her continuing attempts at proper embouchure, and her eternally silent trumpet.

"And Mr. Mixler asked me to come to school half an hour early on Monday," she had finished. "I'm going to tell him how sorry I am for lying, and then he'll probably ask me to give him back the trumpet."

"Good luck, Daughter," her father said now, putting his hand on her shoulder.

"Thank you, Father."

Her fierce raccoon mask was still in her backpack. *Courage*, she beamed telepathically to herself. Then she wondered if it was possible to beam a thought telepathically to oneself. Perhaps self-telepathic beaming was just another term for thinking.

Courage, she thought.

In the car on the way to Lake Harriet, Julia Gillian breathed deeply. She wanted to murmur her invisibility enchantment, but since it had not worked in the past, there was no reason to believe it would work now.

Courage.

Principal Smartt was unlocking the doors when Julia Gillian walked up the steps.

"Well, hello, Julia Gillian," she said. "Aren't you an early bird today?"

"Indeed I am. I have an appointment with Mr. Mixler."

Principal Smartt stood aside to let her pass. She, too, must have sensed that Julia Gillian was a girl on a mission. It was time to face the music, and she wanted to get it over with. It was strange being at school before anyone else. The hallways were dark and hushed, and only Principal Smartt's office was bright and busy. For all Julia Gillian knew, and depending on the punishment Mr. Mixler saw fit to give her for lying, not to mention wasting a school trumpet and his valuable teaching time, she might be spending the morning there later on. There was the long bench where children sat, waiting for Principal Smartt to call them one by one into her interior office.

She made her way down the long staircase, pausing briefly on each step.

Now she stood outside the music room, clutching her trumpet, in its case, in front of her like a shield. The small, high window of the music room door was brightly lit. Mr. Mixler was inside, waiting for Julia Gillian.

She thought of Bonwit, who was probably in his kitchen right now, making his own lunch.

He had called her that morning.

"Good luck," he said. "Remember, I can't play 'Song of My Soul' right. I mess up on the ending every time."

Julia Gillian had said nothing. She knew that Bonwit was trying to comfort her, but his words were not much comfort. There was an enormous difference between messing up on the ending of "Song of My Soul" and not being able to play a single note on the trumpet, and both of them knew it. Now Julia Gillian took a deep breath and knocked on the music room door.

"Ms. Gillian!" said Mr. Mixler, and he flung open the door. "Good morning to you. Please come in."

He pointed the Mixler baton at a lone chair in the middle of the room. Julia Gillian walked slowly toward the chair. She made her steps careful and precise, one foot in front of the other.

"Have a seat, Ms. Gillian."

Julia Gillian sat down, and Mr. Mixler sat on the corner of his desk.

"I'm glad to see you," he said.

That could not be true, thought Julia Gillian. Mr. Mixler was just being polite. She clutched her trumpet to her chest. She should lay it in her lap, she supposed, but she didn't. She looked down at the handle of the case, which was worn and a bit frayed from years of children's hands. How many students had used Julia Gillian's trumpet? Who would be using it after this morning, once Mr. Mixler had confiscated it?

"My deepest apologies to you, Ms. Gillian."

Deepest apologies? Julia Gillian raised her head. There was a look of sorrow on Mr. Mixler's face, and his baton was quiet in his lap.

"I had no idea you were experiencing difficulty with your trumpet," he said. "I fault myself. As your music teacher, I should have been on top of the situation from the beginning. I should have been of assistance to you."

Julia Gillian was so surprised that she did not know what to do or say. She sat there, holding her trumpet to her chest.

"How painful this past month of lessons must have been for you," said Mr. Mixler. "I can only imagine how helpless you must have felt, and how alone."

Helpless. Alone. Yes. This was exactly how Julia

Gillian had felt. She clutched the trumpet tighter but had to look away from Mr. Mixler, since she felt as if she was about to cry and she did not want to break down in front of him.

"I hope that you will find it in your heart to forgive me, Ms. Gillian," said Mr. Mixler. "Music is all about expression, and I am so sorry that you were afraid to speak up."

This was all so unexpected that Julia Gillian just sat on the chair, still holding her trumpet in its case. Mr. Mixler looked down at his baton, one end in each hand.

"Where was the joy?" said Mr. Mixler.

Julia Gillian nodded. Indeed, there had been little joy this fall, and much of it had been her fault.

"I'm sorry that I lied to you, Mr. Mixler," she said.

"And I'm sorry that you felt you had to," said Mr. Mixler. "Things will be different from now on."

He nodded briskly, as if the discussion were over, and lifted his baton from where it lay in his lap.

"Quickly, Ms. Gillian," he said. "Get your trumpet out. We don't have much time before the first bell."

Confused, Julia Gillian opened her case and took out her trumpet. Did this mean that Mr. Mixler wasn't going to confiscate her instrument? Did this mean that she would not be spending the morning on the long bench outside Principal Smartt's office, waiting to be called in and asked to shut the door?

"Trumpet up," said Mr. Mixler, and he lifted the Mixler baton.

Julia Gillian raised the trumpet to her lips.

"We're going to try something new," said Mr. Mixler. "Instead of buzzing, pretend that you are spitting into your trumpet. Spit hard."

Julia Gillian spat into her trumpet. Hard.

Nothing. She slumped in her chair.

"Are you giving up, Ms. Gillian? Do I sense an attitude of defeat, hopelessness, and despair?"

It had been a long month, and Julia Gillian was tired.

"I've tried so hard," she said.

Mr. Mixler nodded. "I know you have. That's the kind of girl you are. But now is not the time to give up, Julia Gillian."

This was the first time that Mr. Mixler had ever

referred to Julia Gillian by her full name, instead of Ms. Gillian.

"I know that you can do this," said Mr. Mixler. "Your embouchure is excellent, and that's half the battle right there."

He tapped his baton on the desk. "Trumpet up."

Julia Gillian felt like crying, but she raised her trumpet to her lips.

"Now, spit. Hard."

Julia Gillian spat. Hard.

And there it was.

Squawk.

"Congratulations, Ms. Gillian," said Mr. Mixler, nodding happily. "We have sound."

CHAPTER EIGHTEEN
Maybe He Should
Try an Oreo

"Well?" said Bonwit.

The morning bell was about to ring, and Julia Gillian had just arrived in Ms. Schultz's class. She lifted her trumpet, in its case, triumphantly into the air.

"We have sound," she said.

"I knew it."

"Mr. Mixler says that all we need now is volume."

Bonwit shook his head. "I need more than volume. I still can't get the ending to 'Song of My Soul.'"

"Oh, you will," said Julia Gillian. "Look at me: I'm way behind you and everyone else."

"You'll catch up."

Julia Gillian agreed with Bonwit; she would indeed catch up. Now that she had sound — even if that sound was still no more than a *squawk* — it seemed as if anything was possible. Mr. Mixler had advised her to work on sound alone tonight, to increase the volume of her *squawk* to *SQUAWK*, and Julia Gillian intended to follow this advice. But she planned also to work on her scales, and if they went well, then she might even begin the much more complicated "Song of My Soul." The trumpet was hers to master.

"You know what?" she said to Bonwit. "Mr. Mixler wasn't even mad at me. He wanted to help."

Julia Gillian had not felt this free in weeks. It seemed

as if everyone around her could sense the change. Ms. Schultz asked her to pass out the Memory Lanes Bowling field trip permission slips. The morning passed by the way most school mornings used to, in a busy and enjoyable way.

And then it was time for lunch. Given the Dumpling Man and his reign of terror, this would usually be cause for gloom, but not today. Julia Gillian was hungry, and she was about to eat lunch with Bonwit, who was undeniably her best friend. The world was her oyster. Julia Gillian had never really understood what this phrase meant — the world as an oyster? — but it was a happy phrase, and she did feel happy.

♪

"How now brown cows?" said Julia Gillian.

Bonwit smiled and Cerise looked up in surprise. It had been weeks since Julia Gillian had how-now-brown-cowed the lunch table.

"It's Teriyaki Tots day, in case you hadn't noticed," said Cerise. "Meaning how now brown yuck."

Teriyaki Tots were Cerise's least favorite hot lunch.

"You should bring your lunch when it's a Tots day," said Julia Gillian.

"Be serious," said Cerise. "I don't know how to make my own lunch. Your parents made your lunch for you all those years, so you learned how to make your own lunch by osmosis. Look at me. I've never even seen anyone make a lunch. I have no idea how you would even begin to make your own lunch."

This was a long speech, and certainly an exaggerated one, but Cerise did tend to be dramatic.

"It's not that hard," said Bonwit. "Look at me. I'm good at it."

He waved his lunch, which was in a brown paper bag today, back and forth in the air.

"You and Julia Gillian are so lucky to be only children," said Cerise, stabbing a Teriyaki Tot and making it do a little dance in time to Bonwit's lunch bag.

Bonwit and Julia Gillian exchanged a look. *No need to let anyone else in on the baby sisters news just yet,* Julia Gillian telepathically beamed to Bonwit, and he nodded. It was so good to be back on track with her best friend, able once again to read each other's thoughts.

"All those weeks of no sound," Julia Gillian said to Bonwit. "And then it only took a few minutes, before *squawk.*"

"You'll be all caught up in a few days," said Bonwit. "And then you can help me with 'Song of My Soul.'"

The Dumpling Man was rounding the far end of the third-graders' row of tables, leaving good posture and silence in his wake.

"Dumpling alert," intoned Cerise.

Her voice was quietly exasperated, and no one even looked up, the way

263

they had when the Dumpling Man first appeared in the lunchroom. The students had grown used to his presence, distasteful as it was. Besides, it was tiring, always being on the lookout.

"Guess what?" said Julia Gillian. "The Dumpling Man's name is Vince Wintz."

"No way," said Bonwit. "No one would name their kid Vince Wintz."

"Vince Wintz's parents did."

Cerise snorted with laughter. Julia Gillian watched closely to see if milk would once again squirt out her nose. Not this time.

"Vince Wintz," said Bonwit, as if he were testing out the name.

"Vince Wintz?" said Lathrop. "Who's Vince Wintz?"

Julia Gillian felt a pang of guilt. While it was true that the Dumpling Man's name was Vince Wintz, no one would have known that if not for her. He was now nearly to their table.

"Vince Wintz is a droopy dumpling today," whispered Cerise.

It was true. He looked tired and discouraged, and his ever-present bag of baby carrots dangled listlessly from one hand. His purple fanny pack was missing, and so was his notebook.

"Vince Wintz needs to branch out from carrots," said Cerise.

"Vince Wintz should try an Oreo," said Bonwit, who had brought another individually wrapped pack of Oreos in his lunch today.

The Dumpling Man stopped now, at the head of their table.

"Students," he said, looking out over the entire lunchroom.

Cerise and Bonwit and Lathrop and Julia Gillian looked at him, but he had spoken too quietly to be heard by the other tables. He stood up a bit straighter and cupped his hands around his mouth.

"Students," he called. "Students of Lake Harriet."

Now the lunchroom, which was quiet to begin with, became extremely quiet. In the month of the Dumpling Man's reign, the Lake Harriet students had learned how to be silent. Principal Smartt was leaning against the far door, her arms crossed over her chest.

"I would like to apologize to you."

The students were quiet. It was not common for grown-ups to apologize, especially to children.

"I've been kind of a jerk."

Bonwit and Julia Gillian and Cerise looked at each other. The Dumpling Man had indeed been kind of a jerk, but it seemed rude to agree with him.

"And I have seventy-six names to prove it."

He reached to his back pocket and extracted the Lake Harriet Anti-Wintz Petition. He held it aloft and drooped a bit more. Suddenly, Julia Gillian remembered what Enzo had said, that Vince Wintz was teased and tormented, which did happen to some students, and no matter the circumstances, that was always an awful thing. The students were silent.

"I'll be honest with you," said the Dumpling Man.

"I had a hard time of it when I was a student here. I broke a lot of rules. So I was determined to do it right this time around."

The students looked at each other.

"But I went overboard," said the Dumpling Man. "I know that now, and I'm sorry."

The Dumpling Man looked around sadly. Julia Gillian glanced at the Vince inscription on the lunch table. Instead of a long-ago boy in knickers, she pictured Vince Wintz as a sad boy her own age, coming to school every day and sitting right here, at her very table.

"I also have an announcement that will probably be welcome to you," said the Dumpling Man. "Mrs. K's recuperation has gone faster than expected. She'll be back on Monday."

Mrs. K, with her dog-head cane and her encouragement of lunch sharing? Julia Gillian's heart clenched with surprise and joy, and she and Bonwit exchanged a look of happiness. Cerise speared a Teriyaki Tot and waved it in the air like the Mixler baton. Around them, the lunchroom erupted in chatter and exclamations.

The Dumpling Man made his way down the row of fourth-grade tables and turned at the bottom of the stairs that led up and out of the lunchroom. He looked across the room straight at Julia Gillian. She could feel Bonwit and Cerise looking at her, trying to get her attention, but she held his gaze. He nodded slightly, and Julia Gillian nodded back.

CHAPTER NINETEEN
Do I Smell Cookies?

"Here's another one," said Bonwit.

He traced his fingers over a tiny inscription on the door of the basement supply closet: Vince was here. Julia Gillian peered at the letters. Pencil, she decided, dug into the wood hard and slowly and multiple times. She and Bonwit were on a mission to find all the Vince Wintz inscriptions in the school. They were keeping a running list in the back of Bonwit's math notebook, with each inscription and its location numbered in order. They had been looking for only three days, and already they had found twelve. Goodness knew how many they would find by the time they had finished eighth grade and left Lake Harriet Elementary forever.

Halloween was only a few days away, Julia Gillian realized, and she had not even thought about her costume. There had been too many other things to think about.

"Want to walk by Bryant Hardware on the way home?" she said to Bonwit.

The October display window at Bryant Hardware always put Julia Gillian and Bonwit in the mood for Halloween. Each year, Mr. Bryant Senior and Mr. Bryant Junior put the same masks and decorations up in the window. Each year, Julia Gillian and Bonwit looked closely at the witch mask to see where its small rip had been taped. Each year, they privately agreed that the witch mask, along with the other rubber masks, was a

bit too frightening to be put in the window where small children would be unable to avoid seeing it.

"Sure," said Bonwit.

A simple question, and a simple answer. They started up the sidewalk and turned right to make their way to Upton Avenue. It had been a long time since Julia Gillian had felt so easy in Bonwit's company. It was good to be back on track, she thought.

"When are your baby sisters — ?" said Julia Gillian.

"Just before Christmas," said Bonwit.

This, too, was a relief. Julia Gillian had not even had to finish her question, which was "When are your baby sisters going to be born?" before Bonwit knew what she was asking and answered it.

"How are you feeling about it?" said Julia Gillian.

Bonwit put both hands behind his back and pushed upward on his heavy backpack, the better to rebalance it. He tilted his head, considering.

"I'm dreading it a little bit," he said.

This was honest, thought Julia Gillian. Grown-ups seemed to expect Bonwit to be happy about the fact that he was about to have twin baby sisters, when he had been perfectly happy being an only child.

"But not as much as before," said Bonwit.

This, too, made sense. Julia Gillian herself had felt great relief once Bonwit was privy to her lunch and trumpet troubles. It was good not to have to worry about what she was thinking, or what she was saying. It was good to know that she no longer was keeping secrets from her best friend.

"Some things I'm even looking forward to," said Bonwit. "Like playing my trumpet for them when they're older."

Julia Gillian tried to put herself in Bonwit's place. There would certainly be many things to look forward to, such as playing the trumpet for the babies, but there would also, no doubt, be lots of fussing and diapers. Not to mention not nearly as much attention from his parents. Witness the lack of lunch bag faces, both negative and positive, and the babies weren't even born yet.

"Do you want to come to my house?" said Bonwit.

"Indeed I do," said Julia Gillian. "Let's stop at my apartment and get Bigfoot first."

They were at the Intersection of Fear. Across the

street, the wood-chip pile was steaming. Winter was on its way. The little white walking man appeared, and they looked both ways and crossed.

"Hello, Bonwit," called Bonwit's mother from upstairs. "Say hello to your poor bedridden mother."

"Hi, Mom."

"Is that Julia Gillian that I hear?"

"Hello, Mrs. Keller."

"Thank goodness you're here, Julia Gillian. Life is better when you're around."

"Thank you, Mrs. Keller."

It was good to be back at Bonwit's house, even if there was no smell of baking cookies and no art projects covering the dining table. Julia Gillian knew to expect this, however, so she was not surprised. Then she had an idea.

"Maybe we should bake some cookies," she said to Bonwit.

"Us?"

"We're ten. We're old enough."

Were they? Julia Gillian wasn't entirely sure. She would have been intimidated to bake them by herself, but then again, she wasn't by herself. She was with Bonwit, and his mother was right upstairs, even if she was on bed rest. And they had been through so much together lately that cookie baking seemed like a small, happy task in comparison.

"Well," said Bonwit. "I guess we could try."

"Maybe we should ask about the oven, though."

"Mom?" called Bonwit. "Can we turn on the oven to bake some cookies?"

May *we turn on the oven*, thought Julia Gillian. But she resisted the urge to correct Bonwit the way her English-teacher father would have done. It was enough that her father's grammatical strictness had rubbed off on her to the extent that she was correcting others in her mind.

"Sure," called Mrs. Keller. "Just be careful."

Baking cookies by themselves was surprisingly easy. They propped Mrs. Keller's Triple-Chip Supreme recipe up on the counter and followed the directions carefully. Both Bonwit and Julia Gillian had grown up helping their parents bake cookies, after all, so the routine was familiar. Bonwit turned on the oven, and Julia Gillian got out the butter and sugar, while Bigfoot watched with interest from the rug. They took turns beating in the flour. They limited themselves to three chocolate chips each before they dumped the rest of the bag into the bowl. Julia Gillian greased the pan, and they each spooned out six lumps of dough. Bonwit slid the pan into the oven, and Julia Gillian set the kitchen timer. They put the dishes in the dishwasher, and sat down at the kitchen table to wait.

"Do I smell cookies?" Bonwit's mother called from upstairs.

Yes, she did smell cookies. The cookies smelled the way they usually did, too, which was a good sign. Just then, the timer dinged.

"Is that the ding of the timer?"

Indeed it was.

"Yum," called Bonwit's mother. "May I have one?"

Apparently ten years old *was* old enough to bake cookies by themselves.

Then Julia Gillian had another idea. After she helped Bonwit take the cookies out of the oven — they were

both a bit nervous because of the heat — she excused herself.

"I have to go to the bathroom," she called to Bonwit. "I'll be right back."

It was a lie that she had to go to the bathroom, but it was a tiny white lie in service of a greater good, so Julia Gillian felt only a slight qualm. The Kellers kept the brown paper lunch bags in the second drawer of the buffet, and she removed the whole stack, along with the box of Magic Markers from the second shelf in the dining room. Her time was limited, and she needed to act quickly. Once upstairs, she brought the lunch bags and the markers in to Mrs. Keller, who was lying in bed surrounded by magazines, books, CDs, and knitting supplies. She held out her arms to Julia Gillian.

"I haven't seen you in a dog's age!" she said. "Come give me a hug."

Oh my goodness. Julia Gillian tried to act normal, as if she didn't notice anything, but the truth was that she had never seen such a big stomach. She leaned over and tried to give Mrs. Keller a hug, but she bumped into her stomach as she did so. Poor Mrs. Keller. This did not look comfortable at all. Mrs. Keller made a face, as if she knew exactly what Julia Gillian was thinking.

"Two more months, Julia Gillian," said Mrs. Keller.

"Two more months," agreed Julia Gillian.

How boring it must be, to lie in bed all day long. She was not the kind of woman who ever sat still for long, so enforced bed rest must be doubly hard for her.

"What do you have there, Julia Gillian?"

Julia Gillian said nothing, but she handed the lunch bags and markers to Bonwit's mother. Mrs. Keller took them but looked puzzled.

"Bonwit's been making his own lunches ever since this heinous bed rest began," she said.

"I know."

"Julia Gillian, are you trying to tell me — ?"

Julia Gillian nodded. It was odd how sometimes two people could communicate in a sort of code. Mrs. Keller was asking her if she, Bonwit's best friend, felt that Bonwit wanted his mother to continue drawing faces of positivity and negativity on his lunch bags, and Julia Gillian was telling her *Yes*.

"All right, then," said Mrs. Keller. "Will do."

She saluted Julia Gillian, and Julia Gillian saluted back. Then she ran downstairs, to where Bonwit was carefully taking the last two cooled cookies off the pan, using the special two-cookie double-wide black spatula.

CHAPTER TWENTY

You Are My Sunshine

"I can't believe they let us go by ourselves," said Bonwit.

They were on their way to the dog park by themselves, with Bigfoot.

"Well, think about it," said Julia Gillian. "We walk home from school by ourselves. We bake cookies by ourselves. We solve our own problems. Mostly, anyway."

The dog park was far outside Julia Gillian's ten-block parameters, but her parents — after discussing it at length and calling Mrs. Keller, who was still on bed rest and welcomed any distraction, such as talking on the telephone — had decided that both she and Bonwit were responsible enough to take Bigfoot to the dog park and back on their own. At least once, that is, for a trial.

"We *are* ten years old," said Bonwit. "It's not like we're babies."

"And we've never really done anything bad."

They looked at each other. Was this true? Had they never really done anything bad? On Julia Gillian's side, there was the matter of eating the forbidden Oreo, and there was the lying about making her own lunch. There was also the month-long secret trumpet problem.

"Well," said Julia Gillian. "I did lie quite a bit this fall."

She might as well call a spade a spade, as Enzo would

say. Call it keeping secrets or call it lying, it all boiled down to the same thing, didn't it?

"So did I," said Bonwit. "I lied about my mother having a cold, and I lied about the twins."

They had started referring to the baby twin sisters as "the twins." They were starting to seem more real, now that fall was progressing and both Christmas and Mrs. Keller's due date were approaching.

"Your mother having a cold was a lie," agreed Julia Gillian. "And not telling me about the twins was a lie, too, but only by omission."

She had spent a fair amount of time lately considering the variety of lies possible in the world, and how some seemed more damaging than others. Julia Gillian imagined herself being sworn in at the Supreme Court in front of the black-robed justices, her right hand on a Bible, swearing to tell the truth, the whole truth, and nothing but the truth. It was a solemn image.

"My lies were definitely worse than yours," said Julia Gillian. "I mean, look at the trumpet lie."

It was exhausting to think about the trumpet lie and its spiral of complexity. The "forgetting" to bring her trumpet, the pretending to be sick, the snort-laughing. None of it had been worth it.

They were now passing the Grace Nursery School garden. The nursery school students were out today, setting out pots of chrysanthemums and planting bulbs under the supervision of their teachers. Several of them took a break to dash back and forth over the miniature wooden bridge. "Doggie! Big doggie!" called one small girl with curly black hair, and Bigfoot slowed down and tilted his head in interest. They stopped, and Julia Gillian loosened the leash. Bigfoot was an old dog now, and he should be able to look at the Grace Nursery School garden as long as he wanted.

"We've both lied," said Bonwit. "We're liars liars pants on fires."

The small girl with curly black hair overhead him and laughed. "*Liar, liar, pants on fire!*" she sang, and the other nursery school students picked up the chant. Soon they were running back and forth over the miniature wooden bridge — "*liar, liar, pants on fire!*" — and the two teachers had to clap their hands to restore order. Oh dear. Julia Gillian tugged the leash. Time to move on.

The dog park was full of dogs this afternoon.

There seemed to be a convention of Great Danes in one corner, standing patiently by their owners, except when one would suddenly lope about like a horse. Julia Gillian, who had once been knocked off her feet by a loping Great Dane, kept her knees loose and flexible in case one accidentally veered toward her.

In the Small Dogs Only section, a Corgi was gamely trying to herd two miniature Dachshunds who did not want to be herded. Bigfoot tilted his

head and watched the action
for a few minutes. As a St. Bernard, he had
never been allowed into the Small Dogs Only
section. Julia Gillian understood the need for
the Small Dogs Only section, but she still felt
sorry for Bigfoot, who gazed sadly in the
direction of the tumbling Dachshunds.

"I love the dog park," said Bonwit.

"Me too."

Julia Gillian had been coming to the dog
park with her parents since before she could
walk.

There was a framed photo of her in an infant backpack on her father's back, standing by the big mulberry tree in the center of the park, with her mother holding Bigfoot, who was just a puppy, on a leash.

"Let's have a trumpet concert," said Bonwit.

"Let's," said Julia Gillian. "We can play 'Song of My Soul.'"

Bigfoot made his way to the water stand. It was a warm day for October, and he was thirsty. He was one of the few dogs who could reach the highest water bowl, and Julia Gillian admired the way he stood calmly, lapping up the water in his dignified way. Her heart swelled up with love for her dog. He had been her constant companion all her life. He and Bonwit were her best friends. Of course, she also had parents, whom she loved deeply, but parents, no matter how close you were to them, could not be counted exactly as friends.

"Look at that dog," said Bonwit.

Julia Gillian turned to see a scrawny black dog with one white paw leaping in the air to catch a flying-squirrel Frisbee. It was a graceful leap, especially the aerial twist in the middle. With a neat snap of his jaws, the scrawny dog snatched the flying-squirrel Frisbee out of the air. There was something unusual about the way he landed, though, and as she looked closely, Julia Gillian saw that he had only three legs. Just as she was squinting in order to see more closely, she heard his owner calling him.

She knew that voice.

So did Bonwit.

They looked at each other at the same time.

"Is that — ?" said Bonwit.

Julia Gillian nodded. They turned around at the same time to behold Vince Wintz, kneeling on the muddy wood-chip ground of the dog park with his arms spread wide.

"Come here, Batman!" he called.

His head was turned away from them, and Bonwit and Julia Gillian and Bigfoot, who had come trotting up a moment ago, all watched as the three-legged dog came galloping up to be hugged. Batman had figured out how to run nearly as fast as any other dog, despite the fact that he had only three legs, and Julia Gillian was impressed. She wondered for a moment how she herself would do if she were missing an arm or a leg. It would not be easy.

When he got to Vince Wintz, Batman did a sort of leaping twist in the air and came down — splat — on Vince Wintz's lap. Then he curled up and Vince Wintz cuddled him in his arms like a baby.

Bigfoot tilted his head. So did Bonwit and Julia Gillian. They had never seen this side of the Dumpling Man. Julia Gillian had always believed that dogs could sense true dog people, and that a dog's instinct for a good human being should not be ignored. She looked at Vince Wintz, who was singing a song to Batman, and she got a lump in her throat. This was a man who loved his dog.

She took a deep breath and walked right over to Vince Wintz, who was indeed singing to Batman. "*You are my sunshine, my only sunshine, you make me happy, when skies are gray.*" Julia Gillian guessed that these words were probably true for Vince and Batman, because they were certainly true for her and Bigfoot. Vince Wintz looked up at her, and his smile faded a little.

"I see you have a dog," she said, before she lost her nerve.

"Yes, I do. His name is Batman."

Julia Gillian nodded. "He seems like a great dog."

"He is."

"Was he always — ?"

Julia Gillian did want to know the story behind

Batman's missing leg, but she didn't want to be rude, so she inclined her head at him.

"He got hit by a car," said Vince Wintz sadly. "We were crossing a bad intersection by Lake Calhoun. We had the light, but a car just couldn't wait, and he came roaring through, and he hit Batman."

"I know that intersection," said Julia Gillian, picturing the Intersection of Fear.

Poor Batman. The lump in her throat returned. It was obvious that Vince Wintz was a good dog owner, and that counted for a great deal, in Julia Gillian's world.

"Would you like to come to a trumpet concert?" she said.

The Dumpling Man looked as if this was the last thing he expected Julia Gillian to say.

"We're just beginners," she said. "But we're trying."

She could not have guessed that she would ever hear herself inviting the Dumpling Man to a trumpet concert, but life was full of surprises, was it not?

CHAPTER TWENTY-ONE

Faces of Positivity

"How now brown cows?" said Julia Gillian at dinner that night.

Her parents looked surprised and pleased. It had been some time since their daughter had how-now-brown-cowed them. Julia Gillian's mother had made spaghetti for dinner, and her father had made his extra-garlicky garlic bread, and Julia Gillian had brought a plate of Triple-Chip Supreme cookies from Bonwit's house for dessert. It was an excellent dinner, despite the bowl of baby carrots sitting in the middle of the table. Julia Gillian was not sure she would ever feel quite the same way about baby carrots, even if they came accompanied with dip, as they did tonight.

"How was school, Daughter?" said her father.

"The Dumpling Man is gone," said Julia Gillian. "But to tell you the truth, he turned out not to be so bad after all."

"That's the way it tends to be with most people," said her father.

"Can I ask you a favor?" said Julia Gillian. "Both of you?"

"I don't know," said her father. "Can you?"

"*May* I ask you a favor?"

"Certainly."

"Would it be possible for you to start writing lunch bag notes again?"

Julia Gillian's parents looked at each other.

"Sure," said her mother.

"Absolutely," said her father.

That was all they said. Julia Gillian felt another wave of relief. She ate a second piece of extra-garlicky garlic bread. She and Bonwit had a surprise for their parents, and now seemed like a good time to tell them.

"Would you like to come to a trumpet concert tomorrow night?" she said.

Her parents looked at each other, then at Julia Gillian.

"Indeed we would," said her father.

"Indeed" was Julia Gillian's particular word, but she didn't mind her father using it.

They sat in Bonwit's living room on chairs that they had brought from the dining room. Before them, in more dining chairs arrayed in a semicircle, sat Julia Gillian's parents and Mr. Keller. Mrs. Keller, who had been allowed downstairs just for this event, was lying on the couch.

There were not enough dining chairs for everyone, so Bonwit had brought his miniature black-and-white-striped chair down from his room for Enzo. Despite the fact that she had folded herself up in order to fit in it, Enzo looked quite comfortable. Her daily pretzelization was paying off. Zap was seated cross-legged on the floor beside her, and Vince Wintz was on the other side, with his dog, Batman, on his lap. Bigfoot sat up straight, with an alert look on his face. His stuffed bat was under one paw. Julia Gillian had set her fierce raccoon mask on the mantel. The raccoon mask had given her courage during a difficult month, and she felt that it deserved a place of honor. *Thank you*, she beamed to it telepathically.

"Welcome," said Bonwit.

"Welcome," said Julia Gillian. "Please, help yourselves to some Triple-Chip Supremes." She gestured with her trumpet to the platter of fresh-baked cookies that she and Bonwit had set on the coffee table. Mrs. Keller reached out and took two.

Even though they were performing for their families and friends only, Julia Gillian knew that Bonwit was nervous. She was nervous, too, if the truth be known. It was only a week ago that she had been able to make any sound at all on her trumpet, and now she was about to perform "Song of My Soul" in public. But if she and Bonwit were to tour the world someday as jazz prodigies, they needed to get used to performing.

"We would like to dedicate this performance to our friends and family," said Bonwit.

"And to Vince, ruler of the universe," said Julia Gillian.

Enzo and Vince Wintz, who looked surprised and a bit embarrassed at hearing himself referred to as the ruler of the universe, both gave her a thumbs-up.

"And to Mr. Mixler," said Bonwit.

Zap raised a Triple-Chip Supreme and danced it in

the air like the Mixler baton. He, too, had been a student at Lake Harriet Elementary. Julia Gillian wondered just how far Mr. Mixler's fame as a teacher and lover of music had spread.

Maybe someday she and Bonwit, too, would be known far and wide as jazz trumpeters. First, of course, Julia Gillian needed to become good enough on the trumpet so that she could add "Skilled at the Art of the Trumpet" to her list of accomplishments. Nevertheless, it was good to have a dream, and she might as well dream large. Why not?

"We will now perform 'Song of My Soul,'" said Julia Gillian.

She and Bonwit looked at each other and raised their trumpets in unison, as they had practiced. "A one and a

two and a three," whispered Julia Gillian, and then they pursed their lips and played the first few notes. She and Bonwit had practiced so often that they had memorized "Song of My Soul," a fact that she hoped the audience appreciated.

As she played, she imagined the two of them on a stage in a jazz club in Paris, with red velvet curtains drawn aside for the performance, and glasses clinking in the background. By the time that Julia Gillian and Bonwit were touring the world, Bonwit's baby sisters would be old enough to sit in the audience. Their parents could sit together at a round table near the stage. Enzo and Zap could come, too, as well as Mr. Mixler, who would conduct from afar with the Mixler baton. This was all so pleasant to contemplate that Julia Gillian wanted to smile, but that would mean losing her correct embouchure, so she didn't.

She and Bonwit met each other's gaze over their trumpets. They played the first high notes without a mistake, then the thoughtful middle, and straight on through the tricky ending.

Don't Miss the Touching New Book in the Julia Gillian Series

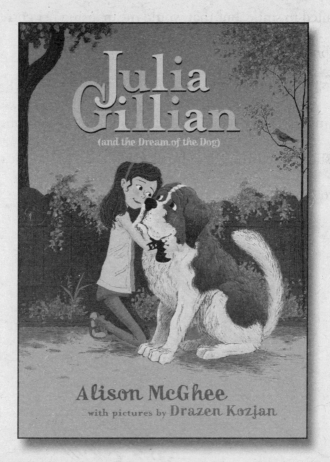

Sixth grade is less than dreamy for Julia Gillian—her schoolwork is hard, her reading buddy hates to read, and worst of all, her beloved dog, Bigfoot, is getting old. Suddenly Julia Gillian's cozy, predictable world feels out of control. . . . Can her family and friends help her face her toughest challenges yet?